News from the New American Diaspora

Illustration: Eli Neugeboren

News from the New American Diaspora
and Other Tales of Exile

Jay Neugeboren

UNIVERSITY OF TEXAS PRESS AUSTIN

Printed in the United States of America

First edition, 2005

♾ The paper used in this book meets the minimum requirements of ANSI/NISO Z39.48-1992 (R1997) (Permanence of Paper).

Library of Congress Cataloging-in-Publication Data

Neugeboren, Jay.
News from the new American diaspora and other tales of exile / Jay Neugeboren.
p. cm. — (Literary modernism series)
ISBN 0-292-70661-8 (pbk. : alk. paper)
1. Jews—United States—Fiction.
2. Exiles—Fiction. 3. Jews—Fiction.
I. Title. II. Series.
PS3564.E844N48 2005
813'.54—dc22 2004026689

For my cousin Manya Gerlich Eisner

Contents

Acknowledgments

The author gratefully acknowledges the magazines that first published the stories—all now revised—contained in this volume:

The Atlantic Monthly "His Violin" and "Poppa's Books"
The Boston Globe Magazine "Lev Kogan's Journey"
Colorado Review "News from the New American Diaspora"
The Gettysburg Review "Good in Bed"
Midstream "The Imported Man"
New England Review "The Golden Years"
New Letters "Have You Visited Israel?"
Present Tense "Stairs"
Tikkun "The American Sun & Wind Moving Picture Company"
Virginia Quarterly Review "The Other End of the World"
Witness "This Third Life"

Preface

Here, then, two stories about the making of stories:

When I was eight years old, inspired by Hugh Lofting's Dr. Dolittle books and Howard Garis's Uncle Wiggily tales, I wrote my first novel. My mother typed the manuscript for me, the top halves of the words coming out, magically, in red, the bottom halves in black, and for several months I would stand in front of my fourth grade class at P.S. 246 in Brooklyn each Monday morning and read a new chapter of the book. My novel, made up of a series of stories that recounted the adventures of a family of pigs, ran to about seventy or eighty pages, and after I had read each new section aloud—at lunch hour and recess, and on the way home—my classmates would crowd around me and ask: *What happens next?*

My answer: *I don't know.* Until I actually sat down and wrote—until I gave myself up to my characters and their lives—I never really knew what was going to happen next. I must have sensed even then what I've learned since—that in fiction, as in life, predictability is as much the enemy of good stories as it is of interesting lives; if what I was writing didn't surprise me, chances were it wasn't going to surprise anyone else either.

Seventeen years later, I was substitute teaching in a Brooklyn junior high school that had a largely black and Latino population, and I was assigned to what the vice principal told me was the school's most unruly eighth grade class ("Just try to make sure nobody gets hurt," he suggested). "You the sub?" a student called out when I entered the room. Yes, I answered, and I asked the class to please take out their notebooks and to begin writing a composition about how they had spent their summer vacations. The students cursed and groaned, several of them packing up their stuff and heading for the back door, when—a survival instinct?—I shouted, "*And you don't have to tell the truth!*"

This stopped them. "You mean we can *lie?*" a student called out.

"I didn't say that," I said. "I just said that you don't have to tell the truth."

For the next half hour or so, the students worked quietly and diligently. I was amazed (as was the vice principal when he came by to see how things were going). When the students were done, they brought their stories to me, I made corrections and suggestions, they made revisions, they read their stories to one another—and for weeks afterwards when I would meet some of them in the hallways, they would ask what I had thought of their stories, and if I would read new stories they had been working on.

The dozen stories in *News from the New American Diaspora* all tell of Jews in various states of exile and expatriation—strangers in strange lands, far from home. But where did these particular stories, and the desire to set them down—the passion to make things up—come from?

Here, by way of another story, one answer: When I was a boy, I went to synagogue each Saturday morning with my father, and when the time came for our rabbi to give his sermon, I would often sneak downstairs to the synagogue's basement and enter a dark, narrow room at the back. The room was called the *Genizah*, and I would sit in it by myself, take down a copy of the Bible (the Five Books of Moses, also known as the Old Testament, the Torah, or the Pentateuch) from one of the shelves, and read.

These were my happiest hours in the synagogue. What I loved most about the book was that it was filled with stories, and what I loved about the stories was that they were about families. The families, though living in times and places far from my life, did not seem all that different from my own: they quarreled, they cheated, they sinned; they raged and argued and connived. Brother hated brother, sister envied sister, wife resented husband; jealousies and betrayals abounded, grudges went on for generations, favorite sons and scorned daughters despising one another and plotting vengeance. They may have been shepherds in the land of Canaan, and we may have been merchants and peddlers in the land of Brooklyn—still, when I read about Abraham and Isaac, Jacob and Esau, Rebecca, Leah, Rachel, Sarah, Hagar, and Ishmael, I felt as if I were reading about people I knew well.

The parts of the Bible I loved most were Ecclesiastes and the story of Joseph. I loved Ecclesiastes, I think, not because I understood it, but for an opposite reason: because I *hardly* understood it. What I loved was the language—the words, sounds, cadences.

> *And whatsoever mine eyes desired I kept not from them. I withheld not my heart from any joy: for my heart rejoiced in all my labor: and this was my portion of all my labour.*
>
> *Then I looked on all the works that my hands had wrought, and on the labour that I had laboured to do: and behold, all was vanity and vexation of the spirit, and there was no profit under the sun.* (Ecclesiastes 2:10–11)

And when I read about Joseph turning away and weeping after he has been reunited in Egypt with his brothers, I would feel my eyes brim with tears. Now, more than a half century later, seeing myself as a small boy in that dimly lit room that smelled of old leather and mildew, what I cherish is the image: a boy being moved by language and by tale (and not by moral invective); a boy who has stolen away, is afraid of being found out, and is lost in story.

The stories I have gathered for this new collection span most of the last century of Jewish-American life. In one story, an American soldier who has survived life in a Japanese prisoner of war camp grieves for members of his family who have died in a Nazi death camp; in another, a family makes one- and two-reel films in Fort Lee, New Jersey, in 1915; in yet another, a Russian Jew living with his wife in post–World War II New England becomes involved with the daughter of the man who has helped bring him out of bondage; in others, elderly Jews, displaced from New York City to senior-citizen cities in present-day Florida, struggle with memory, madness, and mortality. Set in various times and places, these stories all elaborate on the theme announced in the book's title, while also, I trust, telling of that greater diaspora—geographical, emotional, or spiritual—in which many of us, whether Jews or non-Jews, now live.

When I was growing up in Brooklyn in the years following World War II, like most lower-middle-class Jews whose families had recently arrived in America, I lived on the margins of two worlds, one Jewish, the other American. Both sets of my grandparents, and many of my aunts and uncles, were born in that region of Russia and Poland that is now the Ukraine. My father's family (he had eight brothers and sisters, all married, all with children) were Orthodox Jews. They kept kosher homes, ate only in strictly kosher restaurants, and observed the Sabbath and all Jewish holidays. On these holy days they did not ride, write, cook, use the phone, turn lights on or off, or perform anything that might be considered work.

My mother's family (she had four sisters and one brother, all married, all with children) was nonobservant, and my mother was fierce in her belief that religions were the cause of most of the world's ills. Although I attended synagogue each Sabbath and, from the age of thirteen, prayed in our living room each morning alongside my father—first putting on my *talit* (prayer shawl) and *tephillin* (black leather straps I wound around arm and head)—I also, on the Sabbath and Jewish holidays, cooked, wrote, turned on the radio and TV, used the phone, rode the subways, played ball, went to movies, and worked at part-time jobs.

In my neighborhood, distant by about a dozen blocks from the Crown Heights neighborhood in which most of my father's family lived, I was the *most* observant of my (nonobservant) Jewish friends; when I visited with my father's family, I was the *least* observant of my aunts, uncles, and cousins. Thus, not only was I endlessly navigating the borders between the Jewish and American worlds into which I was born, but within my Jewish world, I found myself continually moving back and forth between two very different worlds, and so I wondered always: Which world was, or might be, mine?

It is the tension between these worlds—between their secularity and religiosity, between the rituals and laws of my Jewish inheritance and the worldly (American) freedoms of the street—that defined much of my childhood and that, I suspect, has informed my fictions: What does it mean to be a Jew—and what does it mean to be a Jew in America in the twentieth and twenty-first centuries, and (a question Rabbi Saul Gewirtz, in the title story, asks) how to carry forward values that have come down to us for five thousand years when, physically and spiritually, not only is the threat and reality of exile, as ever, a constant, but when the Jewish community is (or seems to be) losing its essential power and coherence to the riches, seductions, and vagaries of a more homogenized American life.

Feelings, thoughts, and dreams that were engendered in my childhood by living in several worlds but feeling at home in none of them—these, along with the discoveries and joys that came from the reading and making of stories—shaped me as profoundly then as, six decades later, they do now. To be able to imagine worlds that existed before I was born, or that had not yet come into being—to be able to live lives that were not mine, and to do so in places I had never visited—to be a rabbi, a violinist, a filmmaker, a linguist, an old woman, a young mother, a Russian emigré, a devout Jew or a convert or an Israeli exchange student—and to be able, in my imagination and prose, to travel anywhere in time and space, endlessly crossing and recrossing the border that divided the Old Country from the New, the insular world of my Jewish family and neighborhood from the larger American world beyond—this, now as then, both saved my life and gave me life, for the worlds that lived in my imagination were rich—safe somehow—in ways the actual world was not, even if what they were rich in was often misery and madness.

There was this too: my imagination seemed the best, truest, and most real place in the universe because living in it I didn't have to tell the truth. When I was reading stories or making them up, though I might, as here, be writing about loss, I never felt lost. Though I might write about death and sorrow, I could, in the people, landscapes, and tales I created, delineate discrete points of light—moments that suggested the fact or possibility of joy or of happiness.

In recent years, I have published several nonfiction books wherein I write directly about my actual life. But precisely because I am not often aware of where, in my life, my stories have come from—because, that is, they rise up from wells of memory and desire I often didn't know existed until I wrote the stories they helped generate—they are often, like remembered moments of dreams, more vivid and more deeply felt—more intense and resonant—than my nonfiction.

Whatever else I have written since I wrote that early (and lost) first novel—memoirs, screenplays, essays, reviews, novels—I have through the years, as here, returned again and again to my first love: the making of stories that can be read—or listened to—in a single sitting. And sometimes, as in the tale with which this book ends—of a family making a one-reel (silent) film on a frozen lake in New Jersey in 1915—the stories, though lodged in the details of a particular moment, are also about what, first and last, continues to inspire, and what, I hope, will please readers: the sheer magic and joy of storytelling and of story-making.

Jay Neugeboren
New York City, 2004

Note on the Dedication

On April 21, 2004, five weeks before I received the copyedited version of this book, the *New York Times* forwarded a letter to me. The letter had been sent to the *Times* via e-mail by Rachel Eisner, a college student at the State University of New York at Binghamton, on behalf of her grandmother, Manya Gerlich Eisner, who had seen an op-ed article I had published in the *Times*.

"This is a long shot," Manya's letter began, "but I can lose nothing, maybe gain a lot." Manya wrote that she had come to the United States in 1947 and that she had spent three years in concentration camps, where she had lost her entire family. When she was a young girl, she remembered, her father's sister, Sarah Miriam, was getting married. "My grandfather's name was Mendel Gerlich," she wrote. "He came from Rimanov, Poland."

My grandmother's maiden name was Gerlich, and she too, like my grandfather, came from Rimanov, a small *shtetl* in what is now the Ukraine but was then Poland.

Manya wrote that she had, at the time of her aunt Sarah Miriam's wedding, heard her grandfather speak of a sister in the United States who had married a man with an unusual name—Neugeboren—and that she had never forgotten the name.

She had seen my article, she continued, and "had always wanted to search into this matter, since there is not a soul left on my father's side of the family." Would I please respond, "regardless of whether there is a connection or not."

I telephoned her at once, and we talked for a long time. Manya lived in Ellenville, New York, a city in the Catskills about two hours from New York City, where she had made her home for more than fifty years (her husband, Herman Eisner, also a survivor of the camps, had been rabbi at Congregation Ezrath Israel, an orthodox synagogue in Ellenville, from 1949 until his retirement in 1988; he died in 1995), but she was, by chance, coming into New York City the next day for a doctor's appointment.

We met in the doctor's waiting room. "Neugeboren?" she asked, when she emerged from the doctor's office and saw me sitting there. We embraced, after which she asked me to go back into the doctor's office with her so he could meet me—she had told him the story, just as, in the days and weeks that followed, she would tell the story to many others—and then we went downstairs to the hospital's lounge and talked some more. After I had telephoned my children and many of my cousins the night before to tell them the story, I had gone through folders that contained information about the Neugeborens and Gerlichs, and I had brought some documents with me—a page from my "baby book," in which my mother had written my grandmother's name ("Bela née Gerlich Neugeboren"); a page from the 1910 U.S. census that listed the names of my grandparents and their children and provided data about them.

Manya, like my father, was one of nine children. She had been in Auschwitz for three years, taken there shortly before her eighteenth birthday, and was liberated in 1945 from Bergen-Belsen. She had met and married her husband the following year—he too had been in Auschwitz—and she was the only survivor in her family: all the relatives on her father's side—aunts, uncles, cousins, and her eight brothers and sisters—were gone.

Both Neugeboren and Gerlich are rare names—any Neugeboren I have ever met has come from either Rimanov or a nearby village, and for Manya the same was true of the name Gerlich. We talked, and we laughed, and we sat there astonished—"I can't believe it, I can't believe it," she kept saying—as we tried to comprehend our story's obvious, and wonderful, conclusion: her grandfather and my grandmother had been brother and sister.

"Then we are second cousins," Manya said to me again, as she had the night before, after which she talked, very briefly, of the family she had lost.

"Well," I said. "You have lots of cousins now."

This book, then—these twelve tales of exile, expatriation, and loss—is dedicated, with love, to my cousin Manya Gerlich Eisner.

News from the New American Diaspora

News from the New American Diaspora

When the telephone rang, shortly after three a.m. on a cold, early November morning—Officer Ed Sedowski calling to say that a lost Torah had been found wandering around the local shopping mall—Rabbi Saul Gewirtz was fast asleep on his living room couch, having taken himself there some two hours before, following a fight with his wife, Pauline. This time Pauline had struck the rabbi in the face with her YMCA gym bag, a bag heavy with sneakers, clothing, and her two-pound hand weights, and he had responded—a first—by swinging back, an open-handed slap that knocked her to the floor.

Now, twenty minutes later, his jaw aching and slightly swollen, the rabbi stood in the parking lot of his synagogue—Congregation B'nai Israel, in Northampton, Massachusetts—and watched Officer Sedowski unlock the trunk of his squad car. Officer Sedowski, a large, friendly man in his mid-fifties, had been the synagogue's custodian thirty-one years before, when the rabbi had first come to Northampton from rabbinical school.

"Listen, Rabbi," Officer Sedowski said, unzipping a body bag, then stepping away so the rabbi could look into the trunk. "I wanted to let you know right away, because if I file a report, the newspaper's gonna be all over you, and I figured you didn't need that."

The rabbi stared at the Torah, which lay on a spare tire at the bottom of the trunk's well, illuminated there by the faint orange-yellow glow of the trunk-light.

"You could have charged it with vagrancy, no?" the rabbi said.

"Breaking and entering, perhaps?"

Officer Sedowski laughed, and leaned close to the rabbi. "You Jews—always with the jokes," he said. He smelled strongly of whiskey. "No disrespect to my own, Rabbi, but I wish Father Wanczyk had a sense of humor like you got. No matter what others say about you, I say this: anybody keeps his sense of humor given all the shit you've been through, I take my hat off to him."

"Ah," the rabbi said. "Then you know my wife."

Officer Sedowski laughed again. "Only we should get in out of the cold," he said. "You're shivering."

Officer Sedowski leaned into the trunk, emerged with the Torah, and, as if it were a new-born infant swaddled in soft blankets, he presented it to the rabbi. Officer Sedowski was a great bear of a man, nearly six feet tall and weighing well over two hundred pounds, yet he moved with surprising grace, and before the rabbi could offer to unlock the synagogue door, Officer Sedowski had produced a ring of keys, selected one of them, opened the door, and turned on lights.

The rabbi walked past classrooms, past bulletin boards covered with brightly colored drawings, past framed portraits of John F. Kennedy, Martin Luther King, Jr., and Yitzhak Rabin. Officer Sedowski opened another door. The rabbi hesitated, then moved forward into the darkness of the Sanctuary.

The rabbi felt warmth return to his fingertips. He recalled briefly how, even as a young boy, he had felt at home in the Sanctuary. Afternoons, he would tell his Hebrew School teacher that he had to go to the bathroom, after which he would sneak into the Sanctuary and gaze at the stained glass windows—at menorahs and lions, lambs and Stars of David—and imagine the order in which the individual pieces of colored glass might have been joined to one another.

Now, comforted by the stillness of the Sanctuary, he wondered how it was possible that only a few hours before he and Pauline had been screaming and cursing like maniacs. Was it possible he had, once upon a time, loved this woman more than life itself—that he had felt, during their early years, a hunger for her that seemed larger than the universe, and that, this hunger in his loins, he had mounted her again and again so that their awkward and exhausting motions had resulted in the two human beings they now called son and daughter?

Officer Sedowski stood at the rear of the Sanctuary, his right hand resting lightly upon his revolver. "You've been most kind, Ed," the rabbi said. "But I'll be all right now."

"I don't know about that," Officer Sedowski said. "I mean, not to scare you or anything, but we got people in this town who don't understand what you're like, you and your people." Officer Sedowski took a seat in one of the rear pews, a distance of some forty feet from the raised platform—the *bimah*—where the Holy Ark stood. "I mean, we go way back, you and me. That still counts for something in this world, right?"

"Yes," the rabbi said, and he walked up four carpeted steps, set the Torah down on the velvet-covered table reserved for it, and, looking out at the rows of empty pews, saw that Officer Sedowski was untying his shoelaces and removing his shoes.

"Just last week we busted some creeps with shaved heads and a Nazi flag who beat up on this kid who delivered pizzas to them," Officer Sedowski said. "And the kid wasn't even Jewish. Go figure."

"My favorite definition of an anti-Semite," the rabbi found himself saying, "is this: An anti-Semite is one who hates Jews more than is absolutely necessary."

Without acknowledging the rabbi's remark, Officer Sedowski took off his police hat and replaced it with a *yarmulke*. The rabbi heard Officer Sedowski sigh, and it was as if this slight exhalation of air closed the distance between the two men, and that, when it did, the years, too, closed, so that the rabbi was, for an instant, a young man again, standing where he was standing now, several boys and girls beside him, waiting for him to show them what to do when they were called upon to read from the Torah. Officer Sedowski leaned back and, like a child waving good-bye, raised his right hand, wiggled his fingers, and closed his eyes.

The rabbi touched the wooden staves upon which the Torah scrolls were rolled, after which, for the first time since he had entered the Sanctuary, he looked at the Torah itself. The velvet mantle was worn through in spots—as if balding, he thought—though Hebrew letters representing the Ten Commandments, stitched in gold thread, were still discernible. The Torah was small, perhaps twenty-five to thirty inches in length, weighing no more than twenty pounds, and when the rabbi touched the mantle, it was, to his surprise, warm.

If this Torah had ever been adorned with the traditional ornaments—silver breastplate and crown—they were gone. Stolen? Pawned? Sold? According to rabbinic tradition, the rabbi knew, the Torah, like the Sabbath, was considered the Bride of Israel. It was also, according to some legends, the daughter of God. But if the Torah were a daughter, then surely it had been born to marry and to bear children. Yet who could ever be worthy of marrying the daughter of God, and what could the issue of such a marriage be? And, too—he smiled at the notion—what would it be like to have God for a father-in-law?

A bad wife is worse than death. He thought of reciting the old Yiddish saying for Officer Sedowski. But Officer Sedowski was fast asleep, snoring away, his mouth open in a small 'O'—looking the way Pauline's mouth looked after he had struck her. *A bad wife is worse than death . . . for Death only comes once.*

If one dropped the Torah, one was obliged to fast for forty days, though this obligation could be revoked by a tribunal of three rabbis, a *Beth Din.* If even a single letter within the Torah was missing, or marred, the Torah was considered *pasul*—unclean—and could not be used until a scribe had gone through it, beginning to end, and repaired it. Were it not for the Torah, the rabbis believed—and Torah was synonymous with God's love—the heavens and earth would never have come into being. Judah Halevi, the great poet of the Golden Age of Spanish Jewry, maintained that God had, in fact, created the world for the sole purpose of revealing Torah, and for most of recorded history the rabbis claimed that the Torah had existed prior to the existence of the world.

But if so, where had it been kept in the time, or non-time, before matter existed? In God's mind? In God's heart? If before Creation there had been a great Void, and if God was eternal, where, for that matter, had *God* been dwelling?

God created the world because he loved stories. The rabbi recalled the saying that had so enchanted him when he was a boy, and it seemed wonderful to him that this object that lay on the table before him—this most Holy of Holies—was merely a collection of stories that told of the feuds, vanities, precepts, history, and dreams of those people known as Jews. According to legend, God had offered the Torah to all the other nations before he offered it to the Jews—last in line, yet again?—but the other nations had refused it. Because the Jews chose to say yes, God chose them.

Was the Torah, then, created for man—or, since everything in the world of generation and corruption exists for the sake of man (of *humankind*, he corrected himself), was humankind created for the Torah? If the purpose of the Torah and of the world was the same—love of God and in God—and the purpose, or final cause of an object had to precede it, did this prove that the *purpose* of the Torah had preceded the creation of the world, and that the world was created *from* the Torah? And if so, was the Torah therefore perfect and eternal, or could it be abrogated?

When his mind moved this way—musing randomly on bits of learning that floated around inside his skull—the rabbi felt exhilarated. If Pauline could have known the person he was at times like these, he believed, she might yet care for him again.

The rabbi slid the mantle from the Torah and set it to the side. He untied the knotted piece of pale blue cloth that bound the scrolls together, gripped the Torah's staves—*aytzim chayim*: trees of life—and made small, circular motions with his wrists, so that the Torah opened, and its words were revealed.

The kabbalists, who believed that God created the world from those shards of words that exploded into being during the Chaos preceding existence, also believed that though the Torah was eternal in its unrevealed state, it was destined to be abrogated in its revealed state. The kabbalists believed, too, that creation was renewed every seven thousand years, at which time the letters of the Torah reassembled, and the Torah entered a new cycle, with different words and meanings. The rabbi smiled, recalling how infatuated he had once been with the mysticism of the kabbalists, and how, when he and Pauline were dating, by recounting the kabbalists' magical tales for her, he had been able to make her mouth open to him in wonder and desire.

All things are in the Torah—in God's perfect love—and the Torah is in all things. Maimonides, in the twelfth century, the rabbi recalled, had listed a belief in the eternity and immutability of the Torah as one of the Thirteen Principles of Judaism. Spinoza, in the seventeenth century, decreed that the Torah possessed no divine value whatsoever. Ahad Ha-Am, in the nineteenth century, had called for the Torah of the Heart to replace the Torah of Moses . . . and Pauline Gewirtz, née Katz, only a few hours before, and but one year into the twenty-first century, had called for him to replace the bag of shit between his ears with a brain, and for this brain to relay a message to what passed for his heart, telling it that it wasn't fooling anyone any more, that it clearly was *never* going to change, and that it was time it did something for humanity: that it should stop pumping blood. *A little altruism, my husband-the-rabbi—one small loss for one small Jew, one enormous gain for the rest of us . . .*

The rabbi lifted the silver pointer (one was forbidden to touch the words of the Torah, and so one used a *yad*, a piece of silver sculpted into a hand, its forefinger extended), bent over, touched the *yad* to the parchment, and began reading: *And these are the sons of Aholibamach, the daughter of Anah the daughter of Zibeon, Esau's wife: and she bore to Esau Yelish, and Ya'lam, and Korach . . .*

When the rabbi's secretary entered the Sanctuary and informed him that it was nine thirty, that several people were waiting to see him, that his coffee was ready, and that his wife had already called three times, the rabbi was still immersed in the study of Torah. Officer Sedowski was gone.

The rabbi carried the Torah to his office, and set it upon a wooden chair in the corner of his room. His secretary let in a young man named Lawrence Horowitz and, rolling her eyes and reminding the rabbi to telephone his wife, she set down his coffee. The rabbi sat at his desk and listened to Lawrence Horowitz inform him that Lawrence's partner, Samuel Krochmal—also a Jew, though not a member of the Congregation—had AIDS, as Lawrence did. All of Samuel Krochmal's T-cells were gone, his weight had dropped below 100 pounds, the anti-retroviral therapy was proving useless. The AIDS virus had now made its home in Samuel's brain, and Samuel was in constant pain—delirious, depressed, nauseous.

"Nauseated," the rabbi corrected.

Lawrence Horowitz's eyes went wide with rage and his voice rose as he demanded to know by what right the rabbi thought *he* was entitled to mock Samuel's suffering. Then Lawrence covered his eyes, began weeping and recounting for the rabbi the story of his love for Samuel Krochmal: of their life together, and of their desire, now, to be united in death, as in life. Would the rabbi assist them in their journey from this world to the next?

When the rabbi said that he could not, Lawrence asked if the rabbi intended to hide forever behind the idiotic passages in the Torah that declared homosexuality to be an evil and unnatural abomination? Or was the rabbi one of those barbarians who believed that, like adulterous women and disrespectful sons, homosexuals should still be brought into the marketplace and stoned to death?

The rabbi came around his desk, opened his arms to embrace Lawrence Horowitz, but Lawrence backed away, demanding only that the rabbi say yes or no: Would he or wouldn't he grant them their wish—that Samuel not have to live on in pain, and that Lawrence not have to live on afterwards, in isolation? The rabbi said that he was not God, nor was he a doctor, and he would have said more, but Lawrence shouted that he was acting if he were a heartless unforgiving God and a smug Jewish doctor rolled into one, him *and* his fucking Torah. Then, seeing the Torah on the chair, Lawrence Horowitz spat on it three times, after which he left the room.

The rabbi stared at the wet spots on the Torah's mantle. The door closed, he was sitting behind his desk again, and Shirley Rosenblatt was leaning toward him, her perfume making his nostrils quiver, while she told him that she didn't know what to do: every night before sleep, while playing with herself, she found that she was imagining that he—the rabbi—was making love to her. Was this a sin?

Then she was on her knees, unzipping his trousers. He pushed her away, asked about her husband Leo. Leo was a drunken, philandering bastard, Shirley said. A *momzer* of *momzers*. He came home six sheets to the wind most nights, reeking of Scotch, puke, and women. Leo would screw anything that moved—whores, other men's wives, his friends' daughters—druggies, donkeys, sheep, chickens.

"*Chickens?*" the rabbi asked.

Just a little joke, Shirley said, after which she proceeded to offer him a catalogue of her woes. Her daughter Amy had dropped out of college, was living in a pigsty with three whackos, and had herself graduated from pot and mushrooms to crack and heroin. Her other daughter, Jill, two years older than Amy, was locked up in Boston's McLean Hospital again. Jill's hallucinations had returned, and God was now commanding her to slaughter everyone in her family, beginning with Amy. If God had told her to start with Leo, Shirley said, she would have gotten Jill discharged, but luck had never been Shirley's best friend. In addition, her visits to Jill had necessitated frequent absences from work (she had been a bookkeeper for a law firm in town for twenty-four years), and her boss had, three days before, fired her. As the rabbi knew, Leo had been unemployed for seventeen months. So what should she do? What was she to do now?

The rabbi suggested she pray to God for comfort and guidance. Shirley looked at him in disbelief. *Pray?!* To a God that had already fucked her six ways to Sunday? She pointed a finger at the rabbi, as if to lecture him, but then, with a swiftness that astonished him, she dropped her hand, grabbed him by the balls, and told him that she knew just where she could find comfort and that he should stop holding out on her. The hand's quicker than the fly, she said. She still had the mash letters he'd sent her twenty years ago, when they had had their fling. He should think things over. When she arrived home, she would telephone Pauline to arrange a luncheon date.

Why did I let you bring me to America? Dmitry Belsky asked. He sat opposite the rabbi, and the rabbi could not recall when Shirley had left and Dmitry had entered. Yes, Dmitry had been cold and hungry in Russia—and yes, too, he had been jailed for his political activities—but at least when the KGB sent him back home, his children had been there to welcome him, and his wife had been there to nurse his wounds. Now, in America, his children despised him and his wife had left him, and for a black man. *For a shvartze!* he shouted. *She left me for a shvartze!* Why should he go on living? He had a choice, he believed: he could kill his wife and the *shvartze*, or he could kill himself.

"But why do your children reject you?" the rabbi asked.

Dmitry lifted his head. Because I'm a Jew, he said. Because they tell me that Jews enslaved blacks and brought them to America in chains and kept them there.

"But that's nonsense," the rabbi said, and he began explaining the ways in which the propaganda of the Nation of Islam falsified history. Dmitry lifted the rabbi from his chair, declaring that perhaps he should, instead, murder the rabbi, who, having sponsored his exit visa by filing an affidavit of support, was the true cause of his misery.

The rabbi felt himself fall back into his chair. Dmitry stood next to the Torah, his face in his hands. What should he do? What should he do? The rabbi put a hand on Dmitry's shoulder, and Dmitry turned and buried his head against the rabbi's neck. The rabbi stroked Dmitry's dark curls. Dmitry asked for forgiveness. What should he do, and where could he go? He could not return home, and he could not return to Russia. So I am become a wandering Jew, yes? No? Tell me where I should go, rabbi, and why God plays jokes with honest men.

They came and they went: a lesbian couple whose adopted daughter, not yet a year old, was afflicted with leukemia; an Israeli man of seventy-eight whose divorced wife was dying in Israel and who wanted to go there and ask her forgiveness, but was terrified of flying and fearful that his ex-wife would die before he arrived; a fifty-year-old stockbroker, whose father, eighty-three years old and a survivor of Buchenwald, had Alzheimer's, was perpetually incontinent, refused to wear diapers or to live in a nursing home, and so was sitting day and night in his own piss and shit in the son's home; a brother and sister, fourteen and fifteen years old, who, victims of a joint custody arrangement in which they stayed in a house that their mother and father took turns visiting, had begun having sex with one another; a former President of the synagogue whose estranged wife, a convert to Judaism, had taken their four children to Colorado with her to live in a commune of born-again Christians; a woman of forty-one—principal of one of the local elementary schools—who, never having wed, or borne children, confessed to a drinking problem, black-outs, and waking alone on Sunday mornings in deserted motel rooms . . .

Officer Sedowski's head appeared in the doorway—large, round, and grinning—just as the telephone rang.

"I'm sorry."

The voice, he knew, was Pauline's, yet it was so soft and loving that, for a moment, he hardly recognized it.

"Me too," he said, and he motioned to the chair. Officer Sedowski sat.

"I shouldn't have hit you," Pauline said.

"The same."

"But you know what I was laughing about before?"

"Tell me."

"By the way, did you get my messages?"

"Yes. But it's been an especially busy morning. I don't understand it. Weeks go by sometimes, and nobody comes. But this morning . . ."

"I'll be quick then," Pauline said. "Shirley Rosenblatt called about getting together, and I found myself telling her about our fight, and she asked what had made me so angry, and do you know what?"

"What?"

"I couldn't remember."

"Neither can I."

"Hurry home, all right, Saul? Hurry home and let's be good to one another."

"The rabbis say that the world stands upon three things: Torah, prayer, and acts of lovingkindness."

"Well, the rabbis say a lot of things," Pauline said. "But words are cheap, fella—so what I say is: put your money where your mouth is. Listen then. This is what I'm going to do: I'm going to take a bath, and shave myself everywhere, and open a bottle of good wine, and then—since it's still bitter cold out—I'll light a fire in the bedroom fireplace, and when you come home we'll make love in extravagant ways."

"Yes, let's do that," the rabbi said, and he looked down, at his lap, where, he realized, he was becoming aroused. "I'll try to hurry, only if you should grow tired of waiting, you can get started without me."

"Oh I love you, Saul," Pauline said. "I still love you, did you know that?"

"Yes," the rabbi said, and he set the receiver in its cradle, after which he turned to Officer Sedowski and thanked him for what he had done the night before.

"Anytime, rabbi," Officer Sedowski said. "Only maybe it was meant to be, because I had something I needed to talk to *somebody* about, so maybe it was there so it could bring me to you and you could tell me what to do." Officer Sedowski took a long breath, and the rabbi realized that though he could not remember how the fight the night before had started, he could remember the dream he had been dreaming when Officer Sedowski had called: a flock of pink-cheeked angels, their wings fluttering, their golden halos shining, had been ascending and descending in the sky above his chimney.

"I had this operation about a year ago, see," Officer Sedowski said.

"Prostate trouble. They got the cancer all right—I'm clean there—only my problem is I can't get the old soldier to stand to attention anymore, if you know what I mean. So what should I do? I mean, between you and me, rabbi, the salary for a cop ain't much better than what I got when I was working here, but I always picked up a lot of nooky on the side. I was swimming in it, you want the truth—and the thing of it is, with both my parents still alive and pushing their nineties, that means I got maybe thirty to forty more years to go myself, see what I mean?"

"Yes," the rabbi said. "I see what you mean."

"Yeah. So tell me, rabbi—what am I gonna do with the rest of my life if I can't do the thing I love most?"

"You can study Torah," the rabbi said.

Officer Sedowski laughed. "Sure. Like you used to tell me—when you're in love, the whole world's Jewish, right?" Officer Sedowski bit down on his lip. "Only I ain't Jewish."

"The Torah belongs to all people. The Lord gave the Torah to Israel so that we might bring it to others, so that we might be a light unto the nations."

"Well, I found the damned thing, right? I mean, it must owe me something."

"What we believe, Ed, is that if at first one studies Torah for the wrong reason, eventually one will come to it for the right reason. Torah is the basis of all things—the source of all change and renewal."

Officer Sedowski smiled. "You mean reading that thing is gonna help me get it up again?"

"I don't know about that," the rabbi replied, "but as my father said, shortly before his death—'I'm stronger than ever, son.'" The rabbi looked down at his lap, at the bulge in his trousers. "'Now I can bend it.'"

"Yeah. I know what you mean." Officer Sedowski laughed. "I'm not dumb, rabbi. I mean, I *play* dumb sometimes. I could of gone to college, like I told you, only I got Janet knocked up when we were in high school, and the next thing you know it's thirty-five years later. And then . . ." Officer Sedowski shrugged. "She's pregnant again, too—not Janet, but our youngest, Helen—her fourth kid in six years. My seventh grandchild. You got any?"

"Neither of my children are married."

"Yeah. I heard. You got problems of your own, I guess."

"Rabbis are Jews too."

After Officer Sedowski left, the rabbi listened to more tales: of divorce, bankruptcy, and adultery; of drug addiction, alcoholism, and sexual promiscuity; of illness, greed, envy, shame, and despair—and while he listened, he thought about his own children: Joel, twenty-nine years old, a college dropout addicted to amphetamines, now, according to reports, dealing drugs in Albuquerque; and Eva, twenty-four years old, living somewhere in Guatemala, where shamans exorcised Jewish demons from her soul while she, in late-night collect telephone calls, exorcised an astonishing quantity of vitriol on him and Pauline.

When there was nobody else waiting to see him, the rabbi left his office, the Torah in his arms. In the Social Hall, a dozen senior citizens—the Glezele Tay Group—were rehearsing a play in Yiddish. In the library, more than thirty Jewish children—the synagogue's five-day-a-week pre-school—were sitting on the floor, quietly listening to their teacher read them the story of Jonah and the Whale. Outside the library, a shelf of notices told of the synagogue's many activities: adult education courses, visiting speakers, clothing and food collections for the poor, the hungry, and the homeless, regional activities for teenagers.

In three weeks, the National Havurah Committee would sponsor a weekend retreat at a beachside conference center on Cape Cod, where Jews from all over New England would pray and study together in ways the rabbi found perplexing. The courses listed in the brochure were of the usual and predictable sort: Experiencing the Twenty-Third Psalm; Jewish Meditation and Healing; Adding Joy to the Shabbat Table; Body Movement in Liturgy and Torah; Jewish Mantras and Jewish Demons. The National Havurah Committee defined itself as a diverse, trans-denominational network of people committed to Jewish renewal and the enhancement of Jewish life. When the Committee had, several months before, invited the rabbi to offer a workshop at the retreat, he had declined.

The rabbi had always been a traditionalist, believing that without set forms—the persistence and continuity of prescribed rituals, prayers, and observances—there could be no true spiritual life. One could not, as he often said in his sermons, re-invent religion each day, or shop around every few months, as if choosing a new wardrobe, to see which religion suited one's passing moods and/or desires. Only the regular practice of prescribed and age-old rituals—the observance of the Sabbath and the holidays, and of those commandments that accompanied the principal events of a person's life (birth, marriage, child-bearing, death)—could bind Jews to their particular history and identity, and thus ensure the survival of Jewish values and of the Jewish people. Without set forms, especially for a nomadic tribe forever in exile, how could one know who one was, and why one lived, and what life was for?

When the rabbi had taken the pulpit in Northampton, the congregation, made up mostly of local merchants and professionals, had numbered one hundred and twelve families, and the Hebrew School had had in it forty-seven students. Most evenings, the synagogue had been empty and dark. Now, less than a quarter century later, the Congregation numbered over four hundred families, the population of the Hebrew School and pre-school was approaching two hundred, and the synagogue was rarely empty at night, but rather, as now, at mid-day, alive with light and sound, with noise and activity.

Outside, the rabbi set the Torah on the passenger seat of his car and, the Torah leaning against his shoulder, began the drive home. Not one person, the entire morning, he realized, had come to him with a question about Judaism. What he should have done, he told himself, was what he had done with Ed Sedowski. He should have urged each of his congregants to study Torah, not because they would have found solutions to their problems through such study, but simply because it was a good and beautiful thing to study, to learn, and to know.

But how explain knowledge to the ignorant? How persuade those who dwelt in narcissism of the healing waters of lovingkindness? *She opens her mouth with wisdom, and the Torah of lovingkindness is on her tongue.* He heard the words, from Proverbs, and he thought of Pauline, waiting at home for him. Was there, he wondered, a Torah that was *not* one of lovingkindness? Torah that was studied on its own merit was a Torah of lovingkindness, Rabbi Elazar had taught, whereas Torah studied for an ulterior motive was not a Torah of lovingkindness. Some rabbis, therefore, said that Torah studied in order to *teach* was a Torah of lovingkindness. And a rabbi, as he often reminded his congregation, was merely a teacher. That was, after all, the literal meaning of the word.

Perhaps, he thought, like those who had come to him, he too had become excessively self-absorbed. Perhaps, however silly the language, the courses offered in the Havurah's weekend retreat *could* renew one's life. Surely the young people and families who were members of the Havurah had enriched the life of the synagogue. Why so fearful of change, Saul? he asked himself. What of himself would he lose if he opened to other ways of being a Jew—to other ways of being himself? If people were lost—and didn't he count himself among them?—what did it matter which path they chose, as long as they chose a path, as long as they willed themselves to begin the journey.

In his home, he set the Torah down upon the living room couch, then hung his coat in the hall closet. He walked up the stairs, heard music coming from the bedroom, and recognized the clear, piercing sound as that of Bobby Hackett playing trumpet on a Jackie Gleason recording of "Somebody Loves Me."

In the bathroom, when he urinated, and when he washed his hands, he said the appropriate blessings. There was virtually no act for which there was not a prayer, since there was no act that did not, if it was human, partake of holiness. There was even a prayer for the act he was about to perform with Pauline.

He imagined lying in bed with Pauline afterwards, her head upon his bosom, while he talked with her of his decision to go to the weekend retreat—to offer a course in Torah study. Would she come with him? They could take long walks along the beach, they could attend workshops, they could get to know some of the younger members of the congregation in an informal setting.

It also occurred to him that he might inaugurate a series of Friday night talks—he could call it News from the New American Diaspora—in which, each week, a member of one of the synagogue's many constituencies spoke to the congregation. He could invite gays and lesbians, feminists and libertarians, Israelis and the children of Israelis, recovering and recovered addicts, Russian immigrants, South African Jews, Yemenite Jews, Jews of African-American parentage, children of Holocaust survivors, Jewish parents not married to their partners, or without partners . . .

What would Pauline think of the idea? And what would she make of what had happened the night before, when Officer Sedowski had telephoned? And could the two of them—later, later—when they woke again, study Torah together? The rabbis had always been realists, after all. A love without rebuke was not true love, they taught. When the rabbis speculated on how God occupied Himself once he was done with the task of Creation, their answer, at once realistic *and* playful, was that God had chosen to spend eternity in the making of marriages. There were, however, they noted, three things about which God was powerless: He could not, at all times, guard all people everywhere from hunger; He could not cure certain intestinal disorders; and He could not repair broken marriages.

The rabbi entered the bedroom and was about to speak—to begin to tell Pauline of all that was on his mind and in his heart, of how he was determined to change, and to do whatever it took to make their marriage work—but he stopped when he saw her smiling at him from propped-up pillows, a finger at her lips.

Without speaking, the rabbi undressed and joined Pauline in bed, and when he touched her with a tenderness he had forgotten he was capable of, and when she returned this touch in kind and opened to him, he sensed that all was not yet lost. The rabbi and his wife made love slowly, passionately, and playfully, and when he was at the height of his pleasure, he felt a small sound within his chest, and then—why had he ever doubted it would be so?—the angels were there, smiling at him—how else?—angelically, to bear him upwards with them on his journey.

Poppa's Books

Poppa's small library of books was his joy, and when I was eight years old I was first permitted, on the day before Passover, to help him air them and dust them so that we could be certain they were completely free of leaven. We set up benches and chairs in the back yard, and placed long boards on them. Then I went back inside and crawled under the table in the living room—the mahogany table we used only for Rosh Hashanah and Passover—and, from the shelves that were hidden behind the table I took down the books, carried them out two or three at a time into the sunlight, and gave them to Poppa. He smiled at me and placed his books, one by one, on the boards, and opened them. When the shelves were empty, Poppa gave me a goose feather, and I carefully dusted the sides and backs of the books. Then we sat together and watched the wind leaf through the pages. I liked being close to Poppa then, because he was very happy. He said to me that the wind itself was like a brilliant scholar who could glance through many books in only a few hours, yet possess within his mind and heart forever after what it took ordinary men years to acquire.

When the sun began to set, we brought the books inside, and I crawled under the table again and put them back in the order in which I'd taken them out. I had always been proud—from the time I could crawl—to be able to fetch Poppa's books for him, to be able to tell the difference between the various bindings and titles. Often, when he was with friends, in our *shul* or at work, he would tell them how brilliant I was—how, before I was even a year old, when he asked for his

Siddur, I would crawl under the table, and from all the books on the three long shelves, know which book was his *Siddur*, and bring it to him. And when he asked for other books—for his *Shulchan Orech* or his *Tanya* or his *Pirkay Avos* or his *Gittin*—I would, by signs known only to me—by size, scratches, markings, discolorations, stains, and fragrance, know which they were and bring them to him. Before the age of three—before I had learned to read all my Hebrew letters—I knew every book in Poppa's library, and could return them to their proper places.

I loved Poppa's books, and the times I spent with him, listening to him explain to me where he had obtained each of them and what was in them, and why he had placed them where he had, were the most wonderful hours of my childhood. They were times I could be close to him—times we could talk with each other, times I could savor the words of a man who rarely spoke. I remember the large two-volume *Siddur* that had belonged to my grandfather—square books that were full of wine stains on the pages that contained the Passover *Haggadah*, and spotted with tears where the Rosh Hashanah *Amidah* appeared. It stood at the head of the first shelf, followed by the *Siddur* that Poppa used for his daily prayers, and then by the various *mahzors*, *haggadot*, single volumes, and tractates from Talmud sets that he had collected. Alongside these books was the smaller *Kitzur Sheloh*, a classic of Ashkenazi mysticism my grandfather had adored, and then the book I loved especially—a thin, dark blue volume called *The Book of the Angel Raziel*, which, Poppa confided, was guaranteed forever to save our home from fire. When I saw the wonderful black pictures of angels, *golems*, beasts, and bearded prophets leap into the air, I was terrified that, while the book was in our back yard, our house itself, unprotected, might catch fire. I always brought the *Angel Raziel* back inside first, and the following morning, when Poppa burned the bread crumbs, goose feather, and wooden spoon in the bright flames of our cellar furnace, I would, with closed lips, silently bless its magical powers.

I loved also the large *Gemorra* that Poppa, in his bathrobe on Saturday mornings, read before going to *shul*, and a small eighteenth-century *Haggadah* with marvelous etchings of the ten plagues, and most of all I loved to have Poppa tell me about those works on the special half-shelf next to the reference books (the *Zecher Rav*, *Mishpat ha-Urim*, and *Seder ha-*

Dorot)—the books and pamphlets written by men Poppa had known personally. Many of these books Poppa had brought with him from the Old Country—from the *shtetl* of Ryminov, where he was born—and often, when I handed one to him, he would tell me the story of the time the author had come to him and presented him with the book, and of how the rabbis would bring the books and pamphlets to Poppa wrapped lovingly, as was the custom, in freshly laundered handkerchiefs.

The image of these unknown men, all of whom were dead by the time I was born, haunted me, and one Friday when I was five years old—it was just after the birth of my brother, Shmuel—while my mother and my three older sisters were in the kitchen, preparing the sabbath meal, I went into Momma's room, and then into the room my sisters shared, and I took all their handkerchiefs from their dresser drawers, after which I crawled under the living room table and spent the afternoon wrapping as many of Poppa's books—the smaller and thinner ones first—as there were handkerchiefs. When he arrived home from work, I met him at the door with one of the books and then drew him with me, by the hand, to the living room, and showed him the others, now neatly stacked under the table. He smiled, and pressed me to his chest. But Momma and my sisters were furious, and Momma chastised me and beat me about the legs with a wooden spoon, and she screamed at Poppa, as she often did in those years, for having filled my head with his useless knowledge and his vain dreams.

Why did Momma scream at us in this way? She screamed at us for the same reason that she had, in the first place, made Poppa hide his books against the wall behind the mahogany table. In the Old Country, Poppa had been a learned and honored man, and Momma often spoke to me and my sisters of how handsome he had been, of how other young women had envied her when, at the age of sixteen, her marriage to him was arranged. Although Poppa was only nineteen years old at the time, he was already looked up to for his brilliance by many of the older men of the community. In the disputation of Talmud, only the Ryminove Rebbe and Reb Zalman, the ritual slaughterer, knew more, and some believed that, had Poppa's family allowed him to devote himself solely to the study of Torah, he could have become a truly great scholar. In this opinion, Poppa told me, with sad eyes, the Ryminove Rebbe concurred.

But there is no Torah without bread, Poppa said to me, quoting Rabbi Eleazar ben Azariah. There is no Torah without bread. His family was too poor—even when the Ryminove Rebbe offered to raise money to send Poppa from our village to the *yeshiva* in Minsk—to allow Poppa to leave. The Ryminove Rebbe and the *yeshiva* at Minsk might support Poppa in his studies, but, with Poppa gone, who would feed his widowed mother and his younger brothers and sisters? And what of his new wife, and their young daughter, my eldest sister, Rivka? So Poppa continued to work, as a laborer in the tanning of hides, and to study when there was time left over, and when life grew worse for all Jews, after the Passover pogrom of 1903 in Kishinev, and after the more bloody pogroms of 1905, in Kishinev, Odessa, Kiev, and elsewhere, he and Momma and their two infants—my sister Suri was born seventeen months after Rivka—and Momma's two younger sisters, my aunts Chana and Esther, took what possessions they could and left Ryminov and crossed the ocean and came to America.

In America, everything changed. Poppa grew ill during the winter—first his lungs, then his heart—and he lay in bed for fourteen months. When he rose from his bed, Momma said, he was an old man. Momma's two sisters, who had lived with us, soon met and married American men, and their husbands succeeded—my Uncle Ben as a dentist, and my Uncle Jack as a manufacturer of interlinings. They gave Momma money, they tried to get work for Poppa, and they bought a small house for us on Maple Street, in the Flatbush section of Brooklyn.

My sister Leah was born during our third winter in America. I was born ten months after that. Then, five years later—an accident, I learned from their arguments—my brother Shmuel was born, and afterward Momma was different. She looked, suddenly, as old and tired as Poppa. Before Shmuel was born she had seemed to me a beautiful woman, and I noticed that she never looked in mirrors. But after Shmuel was born, the left side of her face fell, the skin hung loosely in flaps about her chin, her eyelid drooped permanently, and she began to look at herself in mirrors all the time.

She also began, more frequently, to curse Poppa for his failure to make money, and to hold up to him the examples of my Uncles Ben and Jack. When Poppa returned from *shul* in the morning, before setting out to work, she would ask him how much his friends paid him for the knowledge he dispensed to them. Such a brain! she would cry out. And see what he uses it for! He did not love her, she would claim—to him on *Shabbos*, and to me the rest of the week, when he was away—and the proof was the fact that he had afflicted her with poverty when he possessed the brains to have given her a life even better than that of her sisters. On *Shabbos* she would nag him to go out and find an extra job instead of going to *shul*. All day he sits and he studies and he prays and he rocks back and forth, she would mock, and what does it bring us but misery!

She came also to talk to me, often, about my someday becoming a dentist, a doctor, or a lawyer, and whenever she caught me with one of Poppa's books in my hands, she would snatch it from me and throw it under the table. Did I want to end up with Poppa's life? Did I want someday to visit such unhappiness upon a bride of Israel? Poppa was a poor book-peddler, and not even a book-peddler. He did not write the books, or make the books, or even sell the books. He merely carried small packages of them from one factory or store to another. And he was so slow and weak, and, in his precious discussions, became so lost on the way, that a water-bearer, the most lowly of trades in the *shtetl*, would, she claimed, have earned more than he did.

When she finished one of her harangues and tried to kiss me and get me to vow that when I grew up I would not be as foolish and poor as Poppa, I would draw back and stiffen. I did not return her kisses or caresses. I wanted to protect Poppa from her words. Rigid, I would think of those times, fewer and fewer, when Poppa talked with me about his books, or took me with him to visit the buildings in which books were made. I would clamp my jaw shut and fix my mind upon pictures of myself being lifted up in his arms so that I could smell the pots of glue and see the white sheets, like miracles, coming off the black metal presses with words on them. I would close my eyes tight and fix my mind upon pictures of his eyes, when he showed me off to his friends by having me read to them in Hebrew. I would think of him in our back yard—the most peaceful and beautiful picture of all—bending over the benches, a faint smile on his lips, while he opened his books to the wind.

Poppa named my brother after his own grandfather—Shmuel ben Menachem—but Momma refused to call him by this name. She wanted her sons to be Americans. She called him Sam, and she made my sisters call him Sam, and I was astonished—and pleased—that in this one thing my father had the courage to defy her. He continued to call my brother Shmuel, and I, of course, did the same despite being hit upon the ear each time I did so in my mother's presence. She also stopped talking to us in Yiddish. Only to herself or to the walls—when she was railing against Poppa, or bemoaning her fate—did she sometimes lapse into Yiddish.

Shmuel seemed happy either way. He loved to sit on Momma's lap and accept her kisses and caresses while she spoke to him in her broken English and called him Sam—and he loved to have Poppa and me speak to him, when Momma was not near, in Yiddish, and call him Shmuel. Unlike me, he was both a sickly child and a happy child—frequently ill, but always smiling, always affectionate toward Momma and my sisters, always accepting their attentions and their gifts when he was bedridden, always trying to please them by helping them clean and cook, by bringing them gifts, by singing for them, by doing what they asked him to do.

But he must have loved Poppa as much as he loved Momma, and he must, even, have been jealous of me—of the fact that Poppa could sometimes share his books and his knowledge with me in a way he never did with him. For though Shmuel would sometimes bring Poppa his books, or set them on Poppa's bed so that they would be there when he returned home from work, Poppa, as if acknowledging Momma's dominion over Shmuel, never remembered to ask Shmuel to fetch him a book.

One day, three weeks after Passover—I was ten and Shmuel was five—I came home from school to find that Shmuel had set up the benches in the back yard by himself, and that he was taking books from the living room shelves, and, one by one, stacking them on the boards. Shmuel smiled at me, his eyes glistening, and told me that Momma had given him permission at last to do for Poppa what I did for Poppa. Momma stood on the steps, her arms crossed. "It's only a game," she said.

I looked up at the sky, which was black with clouds. "But it's going to rain!" I cried. I pointed. "Look—!"

Momma shrugged. "It's only a game he's playing. You had a chance. Sam should have his chance, too."

I stood there, Momma watching, while Shmuel skipped around the benches, dusting the books with a goose feather, and crying out with joy each time he believed he had found a crumb or a piece of dust. When he found some bits of cracker—I suspected Momma had placed them there—he brought them to her and she kissed his face, and told him how proud his father would be when he came home from work.

And Shmuel was so good, she went on—so *grown up*—that she also would let him, for the first time, go on an errand for her. He had done a good job and had finished with Poppa's books. Now she would give him a nickel and a note and he would go to Mr. Krichmar's fruit and vegetable store and get for her some carrots and soup greens. Shmuel put the nickel into his pocket, with the note.

"But what if it rains?" I asked.

Momma blew air through her lips and waved a hand at me. "He'll go for me," she said, smiling at Shmuel.

I put my arm around my brother's shoulders. I pointed to the sky, to the fast-moving clouds. "Bring the books in first," I whispered. "In case it rains. Bring the books in first. I'll help."

But Momma pulled Shmuel from me and pushed him toward the street. "Go now. Momma needs to start supper. Go now, darling. I'll watch the books. Go for me, my sweetheart."

Shmuel blinked. Momma pushed him again, through the opening in the hedges, and she kissed him and whispered to him how much she loved him for being so grown up. Shmuel looked back at me, eyes wide, and left. Momma turned and I thought she would go into the house so that I could start to bring Poppa's books in, but instead she came near to me and stopped between two of the benches, as if standing guard.

She said nothing to me and I could find no words. I placed my schoolbooks under one of the chairs, and I waited. A minute later I felt the first drop on my forehead. "But they're Poppa's books!" I pleaded. The sky was black. I heard thunder. "He'll be angry with Shmuel! He'll lose everything!"

I started grabbing the books and stacking them against my stomach, to run with them. Momma shook her wooden spoon at me. "Then let him be angry," she said. "Let Sam learn now. Let him learn. Do you hear me?"

The rain was falling on my face and hands, spotting the covers of the books. I looked around, hoping I would see Poppa—hoping I would find somebody else in the yard who could help me. "*Please*—" I cried. "It's raining. Can't you see?"

Momma did not seem to hear me, or even to be talking to me. "What did books ever get for us? Look at Jack—look at Ben. Look at the way people look up to them. Do they set their books out before Passover?" Her left eye closed all the way. "Ha!" she cried.

I started to run toward the house with the books, and she moved at last, blocking my way with her body. I tried to get by her, but she began knocking the books from my arms with her wooden spoon. "Sam put the books out—you shouldn't take away from him!" she yelled. "You shouldn't be a bully to him! Sam put them out!"

When I bent down to pick up the books, she beat me upon the back and neck. The rain was pouring down now, and in my mouth it tasted of salt. I looked behind me. The benches and boards were dark with water. The rain was splashing against the books, and I could see droplets springing back into the air, in tiny explosions. I ran past Momma to the porch, dropped the books I still held in my arms, and grabbed a blanket. I ran back out and threw the blanket over one of the boards to cover a row of books. I started to grab more books, but Momma was chasing me now, cursing and yelling, and for an instant I stopped and let her beat against me with her spoon and her fist, so that I could be certain I was not dreaming. Her blows hardly hurt. Then I started moving again, as fast as I could, and she continued to chase me and to shriek at me. Sam would not turn out like his father, but I would, she cried. She saw that now. Poppa would have knocked down a Cossack for her when he was young, but now he could not even lift a sack of flour! Her mother and sisters had been raped while wealthy Jews traded their jewels for freedom! I watched rainwater slide down her chin. She tore at her hair. I found another blanket, but while I was spreading that over a second row of books, Momma was lifting the first blanket and howling the way I remembered her howling on the night Shmuel was born.

Thunder crashed and broke the skies, closer to us, and I covered my head, afraid a limb on a tree would fall on me. My clothes were already soaked through. I stood and looked at the books and I knew that all hope was gone. Momma's body sagged.

Shmuel came running through the hedges then, carrying carrots and soup greens in his two tiny hands. He ran straight to Momma and she lifted him and hugged him. "My precious Sam. My darling. My *bubula*," she cooed to him, forgetting, in her agony, and speaking in Yiddish. "My darling Samela. My love-child. My sweetness. It's not your fault, don't you see? It's not your fault, my precious."

Shmuel burst into tears. I wanted to go to him—to snatch him from my mother's arms—but even while she covered his face with kisses, she glared at me with such coldness that I dared not move. I covered the books again, with the wet blankets, and picked up those books that had fallen onto the dirt and the grass. "Did your Poppa ever tell you not to take his books out?" she was saying in Shmuel's ear. "Did he tell you not to bring them back in? Did he let you help him air the books at Passover, or did he let only Noah? Come with me, *bubula*. Come, darling . . ."

She carried him into the house. I came in after them, with as many books as I could carry, but Momma did not pay attention to me. By the kitchen stove, she was changing Shmuel into dry clothes. The books were dripping. I brought them all in anyway, through the rain. I wiped them with newspaper and rags. When Momma left our bedroom, I went to Shmuel. He was under the covers, shivering. His lips were blue, his eyes were closed. "Don't tell Poppa on me, all right, Noah?" he said, and I swore to him that I would not.

I took off my clothes and dried myself with the towel Momma had used for Shmuel. Then I put on dry clothes. In the kitchen Momma was singing to herself in Yiddish.

When Poppa came home and saw what had happened—when Momma told him over her shoulder, with triumph in her eyes, that Shmuel was only trying to do for him what I had done for him, that he only wanted to please Poppa and that Poppa shouldn't scold him—Poppa's body went straight and I saw a look of fire in his eyes I had never seen before. I stayed in the kitchen with them and they did not shoo me away. I saw Poppa's shoulders spread and I saw his mouth grow stiff and hard, and I thought that I knew, for an instant, the kind of man he must have been before Momma married him.

But then he collapsed in a chair and he put his face onto his arm and he wept. Still Momma would not comfort him, and I stayed where I was, not wanting to go to Poppa until she went to him. Momma looked at me and she did not seem angry anymore. I saw nothing in her eyes, neither happiness nor misery.

Poppa looked up at her. "Well," he said. "So you have what you want at last, don't you?" She stared at him, without bitterness. "No money could ever buy for you what you have received today," he went on. "You are a wealthy woman at last. You are a wealthy woman at last."

I went to Poppa then and I threw my arms around his neck. "I tried!" I cried out. "I *tried*, Poppa. I tried to stop Shmuel! I tried to take in the books. I tried but the rain came too fast."

Poppa stood up, without hugging me. I clung to his neck. "I tried, Poppa!" I cried. "I tried! Please *believe* me! I tried!"

He grabbed my hands, behind his neck, and tore them away. Then he slapped my face, hard. I fell to the kitchen floor. Momma warned him to leave Shmuel alone, but he did not seem to hear her, or to notice that I was on the floor. When he left the room, I burst into tears. Momma tried to pick me up, and at first I accepted her embrace and let her hold me close, but then I began pounding at her chest with all my might, until I was free. I ran from the kitchen. I passed Poppa sitting on the floor of the living room, the wet books all around him. I ran into my bedroom and slammed the door. Shmuel was hiding under our bed, pressed close to the wall, trembling. I crawled under and lay next to him, and I held his body close to mine.

The Other End of the World

I first heard about the concentration camps on a gorgeous summer evening—the last day of June, 1946—in upstate New York, just before a softball game, when a guy in my bunk told me that the reason our counselor Don Silverstein was so thin was because he had been in one of the camps during the War.

On the train ride from the city earlier that day I learned that Don was in the Brooklyn Dodger farm system before the War, and that after a lot of Dodger regulars were drafted, and before Don was inducted and sent to the South Pacific, he had actually played in three games for the Dodgers at the end of the 1942 season. According to different stories I listened to, Don had fought at Iwo Jima, Guadalcanal, Mindanao, and Bataan, had been captured by the Japanese, shipped to the Nazis, and tortured for two and a half years in a special death camp for Jews. Before his capture, though, he had single-handedly saved a platoon of his buddies by hurling grenades into a ring of Japanese machine gun nests. When the Allies won the war and liberated his camp, Don had weighed seventy-four pounds.

Now he was my counselor, and when he stood next to me and ruffled my hair and told me I was a terrific little ballplayer—that we were some keystone combination, as good as Eddie Stanky and Pee Wee Reese—I was a pretty happy guy.

I was ten and a half years old that summer, and sometimes instead of picturing him in his baseball or soldier's uniform, I would imagine him lying on a bed in an Army hospital, under clean sheets, with only his dark, unshaven face showing. He'd be fast asleep, but with a steady parade of ballplayers passing through his dreams—guys who had played in the Majors during the War because their injuries kept them out of the Service, all of them promising him he was going to make it too: Pete Gray, who played for the St. Louis Browns when they won the pennant in 1944 even though he had only one arm; and Bert Shepard, who was shot down over Germany and had his leg amputated but got to pitch for the Washington Senators; and Dick Sipek, who fell down a flight of stairs when he was five and went deaf, but played the outfield for the Cincinnati Reds in 1945.

I saw them walking through Don's dreams and waving good luck to him—not only guys like Gray, Sipek, and Shepard, but guys without disabilities who fought in the War: Billy Southworth, Jr., son of the Cardinals' manager, who won a Distinguished Flying Cross for piloting his Flying Fortress on twenty-five bombing missions in Europe, only to be killed when he overshot La Guardia Field during an emergency landing; Cecil Travis, of the Senators, who got frozen feet at the Battle of the Bulge; Lou Brissie, who had both feet broken and his hands and shoulders shattered by shell fragments in Italy; and Phil Marchildon of the Athletics, whose bomber was shot down off the coast of Denmark, and who spent a year in a Nazi prisoner of war camp.

What I wanted to do that first night when Murray whispered the news to me was to tell him that Don *would* gain back the weight he needed—that if you wanted something badly enough and worked for it with all your might, you could always get it—but I was afraid that if I said anything, Murray and the other guys would make fun of me.

I was the only new boy in my bunk that summer, so that on the train ride, while the other guys talked and laughed about things—teams and schools and the wild things they'd done the summer before—I kept quiet. All the way from Grand Central Station to Albany, where we filed out and jammed ourselves into buses that took us the remaining twenty-five miles to camp, I stayed silent. Even when they argued about baseball players, I said nothing because I was afraid that if I said one wrong thing—if I said, for example, that I thought Eddie Stevens was a better first baseman than Howie Schultz even though Schultz was taller, so tall he'd been declared 4F during the War—they would look at me in a way that would make me feel even more left out than I already did.

Yet I sensed that it was precisely because I was so quiet all day long that Don picked me out that first night, and chose me to be on his team.

We had eaten supper in the mess hall, and near the end of the meal my mother, who was Camp Nurse, came to our table and asked me to introduce her to my counselor and my new friends. When she was gone, Shimmy Kwestel mocked her in a sing-song voice—"Don't forget to wear your sweater, darlings"—but before he even finished his sentence, Don reached across and grabbed him by the shirt, warning him that he never wanted to hear him talk like that again. Was that clear?

So that after supper when we got our gloves and went down to the baseball field, I hung back in the crowd, and when everybody yelled that Don should choose up sides with Rich Ratner, since they were the two best ballplayers in camp, and when they twirled the bat around and Don won and looked around and, having his pick of anybody he wanted, he reached through the older guys and tapped me, saying, "I'll take the kid here," my heart nearly bounced out of my chest.

Although I can recall every detail of that evening—what we had for supper, and which guys were on which teams, and what the baseball field looked like, and which campers and counselors stood along the sidelines, and what happened pitch by pitch and inning by inning—most of all I remember how wonderful it felt simply to be out there on the diamond, on one side of second base, with Don on the other side, at shortstop. And I remember how, when Don stopped talking—which happened whenever the game wasn't in motion—a dark look came into his eyes that made me wish that some day I'd be able to make him forget his pain and his memories, and for a while, that first evening at camp, I succeeded.

In the bottom of the second inning, with men on first and third and one out, a ball was hit into the hole between first and second—a low shot that skimmed off the grass the way scaling rocks skim off the surface of a lake—and the instant the ball touched the bat I was moving full speed along the base path and then launching my body into the air, skidding on my stomach and stretching my gloved hand way out toward the spot where I hoped the ball would be, and then—a miracle—somehow it was there, cracking like a rocket into the webbing of my glove. I got to one knee and threw to second base, where Don took the ball in stride, touched the corner of the bag as he passed over it, and fired the ball to first for the double play.

"Way to go, Joey. Way to go kid—!" he said, pounding me on the back as we ran to the sidelines for our turn at bat. He stayed next to me and started talking fast, as if he had decided to tell me everything he knew about baseball in one long breath, and I stood there listening and nodding, aware that everybody was staring at me in amazement—at all fifty-three inches and eighty-two pounds of me—and thinking to myself: Holy mackerel—I did it! And then: but *how* did I do it? How had I covered so much ground and air with such speed? I don't remember *thinking*. All I remember was that the instant before the bat met the ball, I began moving.

"The main thing," Don said, "is to say to yourself before every pitch: 'If the ball is hit to me, what'll I do?' Be ready. Always be ready, Joey. Be ready for what you think's gonna happen and be ready for anything else—for something to happen you didn't count on. 'If the ball is hit to me, what'll I do.' Got it?"

"Got it," I said.

"You got good instincts with the glove—I see that. Only I seen it before in players. Talent to burn, but without drive. Gets you nowhere fast. Death, Joey. It's death that way. So you play the ball, don't let it play you—the way you just done—got it?"

"Got it," I said again. Then he kept talking about what to do with runners on first and third, and what to do with no force on, with a runner just on third, or on second and third, until suddenly he stopped, as if noticing *me* for the first time. "Hey—are you okay? Let me see—" And before I could stop him he was unbuttoning my shirt, brushing off dirt and seeing below to where blood showed in a diagonal across my chest, like a sash made of red tire tracks, and telling me that even though the scrape was superficial, with dirt in there it could get infected, and that after the game I should head down to the infirmary and get the nurse to clean it out.

"My mother," I reminded him. "She's the nurse."

"Yeah," he said. "Well. You can't have all the luck, can you? Lucky in sports, unlucky in love." He stopped. "Got it?" he said.

"Got it," I said, even though I didn't.

"Who knows?" he said then, but very softly, and when I looked at his eyes I thought of storm clouds moving across the night sky, their fumes seeping into the moon, making it disappear. "Yeah. Who knows about stuff like that?"

After the game, Don walked me to the infirmary, and while my mother cleaned out my cuts, and put on medicine and a dressing, she talked to Don about how happy she was to get the two of us out of the heat and stink of the city.

"You must have a secret for calming my little madman down," she said. "Usually he hates for me ever to touch him. Most of the time, if he was about to die, he wouldn't let me near him."

She laughed and lit up a cigarette, then buttoned my shirt, and led the way to the front porch. She blew smoke rings toward the sky. In the distance, with the sun gone, the lake looked like an oval of black ice.

"You're the one we're going to have to work on from now on, though, mister," she said, and she snatched at Don's wrist so quickly that even with his reflexes he couldn't get away. "I mean, feel this wrist, would you? How come you don't have any meat on you, a handsome fella like yourself? What's some lucky young woman gonna grab onto?"

"Mom!" I said. "*Don't—!*"

"No comments from the peanut gallery." She waved me off and reached up past Don's elbow, to his biceps. "Well, you got strength in there among the bones, only we have to make sure there's fuel too. After all, like I say to Mel—that's the boy's father—the war's over, right? So the war's over, then rationing's over, too. Throw away your gas coupons and your meat coupons, is what I say—it's time to live a little!"

Then she started in about how she couldn't wait for her first day off and the meal she'd treat herself to. Did Don like horse races? If he could arrange it, he should get the same day off she did—that way they could drive to the Saratoga Springs track together, less than fifty miles away. She went on and on while Don stood there, hunched over, until I pointed up the hill, to where the campers were heading toward the social hall for the evening activity. My mother winked at me and warned Don not to think that just because he was so thin he was any Frank Sinatra.

"I mean, when they sent his picture over to Europe, to the DP camps, you know what they did? They sent *us* back a CARE package," she said. "Yeah. Ashes to ashes, right? So get going if you're going. And Joey?"

"Yes?"

"Don't forget to have a good time."

What I couldn't figure out with Don was where all the food he ate went. At regular camp meals, Don went at the food the way he went at ground balls: ferociously. He ate seconds and thirds of just about everything—steaks, chicken, hamburgers, mashed potatoes, corn, vegetables, and noodle casseroles, and he got our waiter to bring him two glasses of buttermilk at each meal.

My mother kept after him, and made him weigh in at the infirmary four times a week. She saw to it that they had the same day off together and took him with her to restaurants she described to me afterwards in detail—New England inns where they served the kind of food we never got to eat at home because we were kosher: pork chops or seafood smothered in cream sauces or milk gravy; salad bars where you could go back again and again to get homemade breads and muffins and marinated vegetables; places where you could have enormous brunches with all the eggs, hash, pancakes, waffles, French toast, ham, sausage, bacon, and home fries you wanted; and diners where truck drivers hung out and they had all-you-can-eat deals for fried chicken or barbecued spare ribs.

No matter how much he ate, though, he didn't gain any weight. It was as if, somewhere between his mouth and his stomach, the food vaporized.

Then at breakfast one morning in early August, a week before Parents Day, I noticed a change—that for the first time all summer he wasn't charging into his food as if there would never be enough of it. During infield practice after breakfast—he put us through a fifteen minute workout each morning once we got our bunk ready for inspection—instead of yelling at us like a drill sergeant, he told us what a great bunch of guys we were and how we'd probably all make the Major Leagues some day.

We were mystified. The next morning, when the bugle sounded for "Reveille," I watched him working out at the far end of the bunk, doing the sit-ups and push-ups he did to start every day. He was back from his usual five-mile run and his T-shirt was sticking to his body from sweat. He changed clothes when we were away from the bunk, and he never went swimming, so nobody in camp, not even my mother as far as I knew—except for listening to his heart and lungs—had ever seen him with his shirt off. But now, staring at his chest and shoulders and upper arms showing through his shirt, I was certain they were larger.

After supper that night, instead of coming down to the ball field for our usual pick-up game, he said I'd have to find a new double-play partner, that it would be good for me to see how I did without him. When the head counselor announced over the PA system that it was time for the evening activity—our favorite: a movie and some cartoons—we put on our sweaters, got our flashlights, and waited on the porch. The guys started complaining that we'd miss the show—the other bunks were heading down the hill to the social hall and Don hadn't returned yet—when I spotted him standing about a hundred yards away, on the road that divided the boys' bunks from the girls' bunks, next to the flagpole where we lined up every morning before breakfast. He was talking, with great intensity, to one of the girl counselors.

Her name was Linda Hausman and she was very beautiful—with large blue-green eyes and long honey-blond hair that had streaks in it that were almost white. She was probably seventeen or eighteen years old that summer, an assistant to the waterfront director, and a junior counselor for Bunk 11, which had girls our age in it. For the rest of that week, while we prepared for Parents Day—finishing up special projects in arts and crafts, practicing skits for Bunk Night, getting ready for different athletic contests—whenever Don didn't have to be with us, or at the ball field coaching, he was with Linda.

He not only started putting on weight, but he began talking with me about how by this time next year he hoped to be somewhere else: if not at Ebbets Field with the Dodgers, then maybe at one of their

Triple-A farm clubs like Montreal or St. Paul. Whereas before I'd been afraid to ask him about his past *or* his future, now he kidded around with me about how by the time he retired from the Dodgers, and became a coach or manager, I'd just be making my way up through the farm system. Wouldn't that be something—if someday, when his playing days were over, I'd be in the Majors, the two of us doing just what we were doing now, except in the big time. "I'd like that a lot, Joey," he said.

Everybody in camp noticed what was going on and when the girls' bunks would call over in unison—"Paging Don Silverstein . . . Paging Don Silverstein . . ." and then, when they got the dining hall quiet, sing the song named "Linda" to him—he didn't even blush. He just smiled at Linda and let the words wash over him.

After evening activities that week, he and Linda would linger behind the rest of us, holding hands, and when they did, I thought I could feel how wonderful he felt—and after "Taps" I'd lie in my bed and try to imagine how she would talk to him and give him back the confidence to believe in himself so he could still have the thing he loved most in the world and thought he had lost.

He might never fully get back the raw physical strength he'd once had, but he could compensate with drive and hustle and—most of all—with knowledge. Nobody in the world, I believed, not even Leo Durocher, the Dodger manager, *knew* more about baseball than Don. Power isn't everything anyway, Don, I imagined her saying. It's being able to hit the ball where it's pitched—it's mental toughness—it's not how much you weigh, but the speed and snap of your wrists when you connect with the ball—it's in concentration and follow-through—it's in saying to yourself before every pitch: If the ball is hit to me, what'll I do . . .

I got to play second base on the camper-waiter team that went against the counselors on Parents Day, and I was thrilled, not just because Don picked me, but because nobody objected. I was the only guy on the field under thirteen years old, a good six inches shorter than anyone else. My father was up from New York for the weekend, and when I led off the game with a line-drive single over Don's head into left field and everybody cheered, I felt as high as the center field flagpole at Ebbets Field.

The counselors beat us 8 to 7, and after the game I saw Don with Linda, her introducing him to a man and a woman I assumed were her parents. Then I saw another man standing nearby, and Don took his hand and brought the man to Linda. Despite the fact that it was a broiling August day, the man wore a dark black double-breasted suit and a black hat. He was unshaven and there was something wrong with the way he held his head to the side—as if it was too heavy for his body and might fall off. His arm stayed bent at the elbow, and he never seemed to open his eyes so that I kept imagining his eyes were somehow unshaven too, flecked with hundreds of tiny black dots, like hairs that were starting to grow through.

My father said my mother was waiting, that we didn't have much time—his bus was leaving for the train station in thirty minutes. I told him what Don said about me making the Dodgers some day and him being my coach. I thought that bringing in the fact that Jake Pitler, one of the Dodger coaches, was Jewish, would make my father happy, but he just snapped at me that he didn't have time to talk about nonsense when my mother was waiting. Then, at the infirmary, my father told me to leave her alone because this was when she had to make her tips. My mother was there, smiling brightly at all the parents and looking gorgeous in her nurse's uniform, her white starched cap on her head like a tiara.

When my father pointed to his watch, my mother excused herself and took us into a back room they used for kids who caught contagious diseases. I tried to talk about Don again—to ask my mother if the man who visited him was Don's father, but my mother and father didn't have time for anything except to argue with each other. When my mother tried to kiss him good-bye, he pushed her away and had a sour expression on his mouth that made me want to blast him with a baseball bat. And when my mother reacted by nagging him the way she always did, about how she'd like to be one of the women who could send her son away to camp and go on a *real* vacation, and why was he such a nothing—"You're a nothing, Mel, and that's all there is to it," she said. "It's the one thing you're good at—nothing!"—I wanted to whack her also.

But what I wanted to do and what I did were two different things. What I did was to wait until they took a break from fighting, and then, very quickly, I said the words I was thinking: "Why don't you both just shut up already."

My father slapped me across the cheek, fast and hard, and when my mother bent over and tried to kiss me, telling my father that he was a bully too, I got away from her fast. "*I hope you both drop dead!*" I shouted, and I ran from the room, heading for the woods behind the baseball field.

After Parents Day was over and camp went back to normal, I threw myself into activities—baseball, basketball, volleyball, tennis, swimming, ping-pong—whatever there was—like the madman my mother said I was. I got into four fights in the next day, all with older guys, but I didn't care, and when Don took me aside after I'd roughed somebody up by barreling into home plate, I shrugged him off too, telling him to leave me alone, to go take a hike in the woods with his girlfriend.

He grabbed me by the shoulder then, and marched me straight down to the infirmary and handed me to my mother, saying he wanted to know what the hell had gotten into me since Sunday. My mother sighed, told me to stay put or else, and then she motioned to Don to go for a walk with her. That burned me even more, because I didn't want him knowing about how my parents didn't get along, and how it was such a relief for them to be apart every summer.

But sitting alone on the infirmary porch, I was scared my mother might begin acting cold to me the way she did to my father, and scared, too, that knowing about my mother and father might make Don afraid of being in love with Linda. I tried to imagine Don joking with Linda about how he'd lost his appetite all right, the way you were supposed to when you fell in love, but that something was wrong, because instead of losing weight the way people in love usually did, he was *gaining* weight. When I pictured Linda reacting to him, though, from the puzzled expression on her face I could see that Don's joke had fallen flat.

"You really love Don a lot, don't you," my mother said when she returned.

I shrugged.

"I don't mean love like with men and women—the mushy stuff like in the movies—but something else."

"I don't know," I said. "I have to get back to my bunk for general swim."

"Your father means well," my mother said then. "He called last night—I meant to tell you before—to say he was sorry and that next time he visits he wants to hear all about Don from you. He said you played a terrific game. Your father's very proud of you, you know, only he doesn't know how to show it sometimes."

I shrugged, and looked at the floor.

"He was almost a lawyer, did you know that? When I met him he was scheduled to go to Brooklyn Law School like his brother Harry. Your father was some smart man once upon a time." She laughed. "We had lots of swell times, Joey. He was the first guy I ever went out with who won every argument we had. Oh yeah, when it came to arguing, your father was the champ." She laughed again, but to herself this time. "Maybe he still is, in a way. Only what happened was his mother died two days before classes started, and when the week of *shiva* was over, he just never went down to school to register. He never said why either. So go figure. It's sixteen years and mum's still the word. At the time, he offered to let me out of our engagement without having to give back the ring, but the day after our wedding I moved in to help him take care of his father and his two kid brothers. Sure. With my eyes wide open I was dreaming, like always."

"Don will be angry if I'm late for swim," I said.

"Shush. I'm telling you something, so listen for once in your life."

"I always listen," I said.

"Sure you do, Joey. Maybe that's your trouble." She sighed. "You just be careful, okay? That's all I mean to say. I think it's good you look up to somebody like Don for a friend. But be careful he don't break your heart." I started down the steps, her voice following me. "You're a very strong boy, Joey," she said, "willful to beat the band, and where you get it from, God only knows, only nobody I ever met got the strength to stop a broken heart, you know what I mean? So you remember that."

By the time I changed into my bathing suit and walked down to the waterfront, general swim was almost over. Everybody was too busy splashing around and dunking one another to notice me. One of the waterfront counselors told me I was buddies with Number 27—

Murray and Alan—that they were out by the raft in the deep area. I dove in and swam out just as the whistle went off. When we were done counting off, I did a surface dive to the bottom of the lake, and then swam back up and under the raft, and decided to stay there.

There was an air pocket about a foot high, and a faint smell of gasoline, from the oil barrels that held the raft up. The air under the raft was usually thick and heavy from the heat trapped there, but for some reason, even though the sun had been shining down on it all day long, it seemed light and cool to me.

The next thing I remember is that everything was totally still and I was having a hard time breathing. I felt as if somebody had clamped enormous hands around my chest and squeezed all the air out of it, the way you squeezed air out of a football bladder before inflating it. I was holding onto one of the barrels so tight I'd scraped rust under my fingernails. Still, I couldn't figure out how I could have fallen asleep while my body was standing straight up in the water, and I also couldn't figure out how things had become so quiet without me noticing the difference. The sunlight, filtering down through the slats of wood, made lines across my forearm, the way light did through venetian blinds.

I ducked my head down and swam underwater for a few feet, then rose to the surface. The swimming area was totally deserted: no campers, no counselors. The rowboats and canoes were tied up at the side of the docks, and the boathouse door was closed. The sun was still high in the sky, so I figured it must not be suppertime yet. I lay on my back, took in some water and sprayed it out in a high arcing stream. I had the whole lake to myself! I closed my eyes and saw sunspots on the insides of my eyelids—like bursts of anti-aircraft flak—and I pictured my mother getting the news that I was missing. I saw her running toward the lake, one hand holding down her nurse's cap, and she was screaming my name, only no sound came from her mouth.

I spread my arms and legs out as far as I could so that there was an imaginary circle around me that was perfectly round, and I thought of a picture I'd seen in the Dodger yearbook of Pee Wee Reese, Pete Reiser, and their wives horsing around in a swimming pool during spring training at Vero Beach, Florida. I began going through a game in my mind too, batter by batter, me and Don and the rest of the Dodgers against the Yankees in the seventh game of the World Series, Hal Gregg on the mound for us and "Spud" Chandler pitching for them.

I heard a splashing sound, and then another, and I saw two people racing from the shore toward me, their arms and legs churning the water into pale blue foam, and I realized that the instant before I heard the splashing, I'd also heard them laughing. I took a deep breath, slipped under the surface, and came up below the raft.

"I won!"

"Says who?"

"Says me."

I recognized the girl's voice at once—it was Linda—but I couldn't tell who the man was. The two of them hoisted themselves up, the raft wobbled, and I heard him ask her what his penalty was for losing. Then the raft shook some more and they were in the water again. I let go of the barrel, and began swimming underwater. Sunlight lit up the lake so that I could see almost all the way to where the boats were lined up. A school of minnows headed toward me, then reversed direction and disappeared. I saw Linda swimming underwater too, gliding in slow motion. She was wearing her black one-piece lifeguard's bathing suit, and her gold and white hair streamed out behind her, as if there were strands of tinsel in it. She was doing the breaststroke, using her long legs in powerful frog kicks, a steady stream of bubbles rising from her mouth.

The other swimmer was Marty Reiss, the waterfront director. He swam toward Linda, and when they were only about a yard apart they kind of pivoted, as if they were lying on an invisible platform that was rotating slowly at a slight, tilted angle, and then they moved forward some more, and, without moving their arms, hands, or legs, they kissed, and while they kissed, they kept turning slowly in their slanted circle.

I dove down deeper, reversed direction, and when I came up for air, underneath the raft again, I was gasping so hard from having held my breath, I was sure they'd discover me. By the time I took a chance to come back out from under the raft, though, they were gone—way out in the middle of the lake on their backs, gliding side by side in long easy strokes that made two clean white slits in the water's surface.

When I got back, Don was furious with me. He asked if I knew how worried and scared I could have made my mother, but I didn't answer.

He asked if I knew how dangerous it was to be in the lake alone and he asked lots of other things, but I just kept my mouth shut. I knew exactly what I was going to do.

He docked me from evening activity—a campfire where Uncle Irv, the head counselor, told ghost stories—and when he and the guys came back at nine o'clock, talking about how great it was, I pretended to be asleep. At 11:15, when Don came in to go to bed, I was still up. I kept myself awake by going over baseball lineups in my head, one team after the other, from first base to second to short to third, to left field to center to right to catcher to pitcher. After I'd gone through all sixteen teams I began making lists of players who'd been in the service and had come back, beginning with big stars like Bob Feller, Ted Williams, Hank Greenberg, Howie Pollet, Ewell Blackwell, and Johnny Schmitz, and then going on to less famous guys who'd survived, like Ed Head, Bob Klinger, Gene Hermanski, Lonny Frey, and Don Kolloway.

When I was sure Don was asleep, I got out of bed, went into the bathroom, and dressed. It was ten after twelve. I took my flashlight, put on a sweater and my baseball cap, and then tiptoed to Don's bed, reached up to the shelf of stuff he kept above him, just under the window, took his Army knife, and stuck it into my belt. I went out onto the porch, where I sat on the steps to put my sneakers on. I was ready.

I walked toward the girls camp, and it felt wonderful to be all alone out there, in the middle of the night, with everybody else fast asleep. The stars were shining so brightly that even though there was hardly any moon, I didn't need to use my flashlight. I headed straight for Bunk 11.

The door squeaked, but none of the girls stirred. I moved the beam of my flashlight around the room, low, and found Linda where I thought she'd be, by the door. She was sleeping on her side, one pillow under her head and another pillow in her arms. Her mouth was open and a strand of honey-colored hair lay across her bottom lip.

I stood by the side of her bed for a few seconds, reminding myself of all Don had gone through during the war, and then I touched Linda's neck lightly with the point of the knife, as if I were poking it into the skin of a fish.

"Don't make a move or say anything or you're dead," I said.

She smiled at me and stretched her arms out. "Hi, Joey," she said back, and there was no fear at all in her voice. She hugged her pillow and flopped onto her stomach.

"I mean business," I whispered. "Get up now. We have to talk."

She rubbed her eyes and smiled again, but I wasn't fooled. I flashed the knife at her, toward her eyes. "I'm serious," I said. "Move it."

"What the hell—?" She sat up. "Hey—get out of here with that—!"

"Be quiet and do as I say and you won't be harmed," I said, and then: "I was there. I saw you today in the lake—what you did underwater with him. I was there."

"What are you—crazy or something?" She swung at me, to knock the knife away, and I saw a ribbon of red, like silk, unfurl from the side of her hand.

"This is Don's knife, from the Army, and it's very sharp. I'll *make* you listen if I have to. Do you hear me?"

She sat there, her hand on her pillow, the blood dripping and spreading. "Jesus," she said. "My hand."

She reached to the side of her bed and took a polo shirt from a bundle of clothes next to the wall, wrapped it around her hand, pulled the knot tight with her teeth.

"If you don't move, I'll—"

"You'll what, big shot?" She lifted her hand above her shoulder, to slow down the bleeding, then mimicked me: "I-saw-you-there. I-saw-you-there-with-him. So what? It's a free country, ain't it?"

"I don't want to do this," I said.

"Then don't." She laughed. Some of the girls were stirring now, sitting up and rubbing their eyes and staring. "You're probably a coward just like him. The way he hides behind his famous wounds, waiting for the world to wave a magic wand. The two of you deserve each other. *Baseball baseball baseball. Joey Joey Joey.* It's all I ever hear and it makes me sick already, so you get out of here fast, you little pipsqueak, or I'll wake the whole camp and tell your mother too."

Then I said the words I'd been saving: "*You have to love him and not another.*" The smile went out of her face, and I kept talking, pressing the words out of my memory and into the air. "That's the only hope. You can't kill him again. You *have* to love him."

She unwrapped her polo shirt, lifted her hand to her mouth, and sucked the blood. "Shit," she said. "I'll probably have to get your mother to look at this in the morning. Maybe she'll give me a note at least, so I can get out of waterfront duty for a few days." She laughed. "I *have* to love him? That's a new one. It really is. Wait till Marty hears that. I mean, I bet Don's a great counselor to you little boys, but what a drip, the way he moons around all the time, always asking me What-can-I-do-to-make-you-happy? What-can-I-do-to-make-you-happy? I'm sick to death of it already."

She laughed again and when she did I felt my heart explode. "*Don't you make fun of him, do you hear?*" I screamed, and I lifted Don's knife and plunged it down toward her mouth, to wipe out her smile.

Behind me the girls were all screaming. Feathers started to float up into the room, and for a second the world seemed to have turned upside down, the feathers moving in slow motion as if rising in water, and me dizzy and sinking into an endless white sky. Linda was out of her bed, backed up against the door.

I turned in a circle and crouched down. "I mean what I say," I said, but I was trembling, and I knew Linda could see that I was. "I warned you. I—I gave you your chance."

"This isn't happening," she said to me then. "Tell me this isn't happening, Joey, okay? Tell me we're dreaming, yeah?"

The other counselor, Marcia Cohen, came toward me but I flashed my knife at her and she backed off.

Linda sighed. "Okay. Everybody back to sleep," she said. "Everybody back to sleep, and fast, or you'll lose your canteen privileges for the rest of the week."

She kicked the door open. "Come on, you—"

I followed her onto the porch. "So what do you want me to do?" she asked.

"I told you before. You have to love him—why don't you just love him so that—so that everything will stop being wrong?" I was shivering so badly by this time that I could hardly get the words out. I stared at the handle of the knife and imagined olive green paint being baked onto metal in a war factory: onto knives and pistols, machine guns, bazookas, compasses, jeeps, tanks. "He nearly died for you and for me. He was in a death camp for Jews—"

"A *what—?*"

She smiled then in a way that made me feel as if I didn't matter, as if nothing I had done mattered, and so I said the only thing I could think of that might still hurt her, the only thing I had left to say: "Okay for now," I said. "But some day I'm going to write down everything that happened and everything you did to him, and then the whole world will know. Maybe I can't make you love him, but I can make you and everybody else remember what happened. Do you hear what I'm saying? *Do you? Do you?*"

I was shouting and crying at the same time. "You are really nuts for a kid your age," she said. "Totally screwy. Listen—you better get away fast before your mother has to strap you into a car and take you to the funny farm. You better—"

"Let's go, Joey."

Don was standing a few feet behind her, and I didn't know how long he had been there. Linda turned. "Oh Jesus," she said. "Oh shit and a half."

"Say it now," I said to her. "Say it now if you're so brave. Say it to his face. Come on—I dare you."

"Let's go, Joey," Don said again.

"Look," she said to Don. "Would you get this kid back and we'll talk in the morning?"

Don put his arm around me. "Let's go, Joey."

That was the night Don told me about the concentration camps, and how he had not been in one of them. But the man who visited him on Parents Day had, and that was what made Don so bitter, he said: that while he was rotting away in a POW camp on an island in the South Pacific, his grandparents and aunts and uncles and cousins, all his relatives except for one—the man I had seen, his uncle Heshl—had been dying in a concentration camp in Poland. What he didn't understand—what would keep him angry the rest of his life, he said—was why God had chosen to send him to the other end of the world when his parents' parents and their brothers and sisters and children—people he had never met and never would meet—needed him on this side of the world.

We sat on the porch of our bunk until the sun rose from the hills on the other side of the lake, and he told me what he knew about what happened to Jews during the war. But he had not known about the camps until he was discharged from a veteran's hospital after the war was over, he said. He never mentioned Linda's name, and he never mentioned what I had done.

The next summer my mother and I went to a different camp, in the Berkshires, not far from Tanglewood. All winter long that year I looked for Don's name in articles about the Dodgers and their minor league teams, but I never found it. Then, three years later, a few weeks before we left for camp—this time to upstate New York, near Poughkeepsie—my mother came into my room when she got home from work at the hospital and said she had some sad news for me: one of my best friends had passed away. She had heard about it from a woman who worked in the camp office the year we had been there: Don Silverstein was dead. He was twenty-nine years old.

When she put her hands on my shoulders and told me she knew what I was feeling, I turned and screamed at her to get out and leave me alone, to just leave me alone! What I kept thinking after she left, though—what I wanted to explain to her—was not about Don, but about what he had said to me that night about not taking things like the death camps personally. The big mistake people made, he said, was to reduce everything to just friends and family, or to who had lived and who had died. The fact that he had never even met the family he lost—"Hey, in what way do we ever truly know another person anyway?" I remembered him asking me—seemed to prove his point for him.

All the things he and I and about a hundred and fifty other Jews had done and felt during one summer in a sleepaway camp on a beautiful lake by a small town in upstate New York, then, were things millions of Jews I had never known and would never meet would never do again. I understood that much. But who were they, and how would the things Don told me ever help me understand what it meant that they were gone?

For a while after Don told me his story that night I went around trying to imagine what seemed unimaginable—lists of dead and lost people that might somehow add up: everybody in Brooklyn; every baseball player who ever played; every Jew in the United States; every person I had ever met or seen—in school, on subways, in camp, and on family trips; every person who made up the populations of entire states and nations—Montana or Rhode Island, New Zealand or Norway—but I could never concentrate long enough on individual faces to get very far.

The news itself didn't surprise me, and maybe that—the feeling that my belief in the inevitability of Don's death had somehow helped *cause* it—was part of why I reacted the way I did to my mother. Realizing this, though, I could also feel that I understood why Don was so bitter about having spent the war in the wrong camp.

What surprised me, though—what made me come out of my room later that day and apologize to my mother for not letting her comfort me—was how much I kept thinking not about Don being dead—I never even tried to imagine what his body might have looked like at the end—but about the way he had seemed so happy for those nine or ten days when he was in love with Linda and when he talked about making it back to the Dodgers. When I imagined him smiling at me, I wanted to smile back, but I found that I couldn't, because what his smile made me feel most of all was how much he had existed in my feelings and imagination, and how little, truly, I had ever known him.

Good in Bed

The big difference between the two great cognitive hierarchies, it seemed clear to him—and he imagined explaining this to his graduate seminar later that week—lay in the broad demarcation between the "perisylvian brain" of language, and the dorsally located association areas that probably underlay both mimetic representation *and* reproductive memory. But was it also possible that the very highest levels of the mimetic and linguistic systems within the brain were bilaterally organized? And was it possible, too, that he was mad to be musing on the origins of consciousness while Claire sat across the room from him, propped up on pillows in the center of their queen-sized bed, and explained to him the reasons she would, the following afternoon, be filing for divorce.

In the seventeenth century, he recalled, the word consciousness was synonymous with conscience, so that Hamlet's line (a possible epigraph for his new book?), "conscience doth make cowards of us all," meant that consciousness did.

"So I'm a coward," he said.

"Oh Phil," she said, shaking her head. "I said no such thing. Do you see what I mean? How you *never* listen? What I was saying was only that you are not the man I married. We've *changed*, Phil—"

"Evolved," he said.

"All right—*evolved*, then." She closed her eyes, and spoke words he assumed she had been rehearsing for some time: "But-the-truth-is-that-the-person-I-loved-once-upon-a-time-and-married-is-not-the-person-I-am-married-to-now." She opened her eyes and smiled at him winningly, as if, he thought, she were being introduced to him for the first time at a faculty party. "And I'm doubtless not the person you loved once upon a time either. If I've disappointed you, I'm sorry."

"Disappointed is hardly the word."

"You're angry with me, aren't you?" she stated.

"Angry?" He shrugged. "Why would I be angry?"

"I've thought about this for a long time and, as I said before, I want to be direct and up front with you." Like a schoolgirl trying to earn her teacher's praise for good behavior, Claire now sat up straight and clasped her hands in front of her. Phil watched her mouth move, but while she spoke he found himself smiling at the words that appeared on the screen inside his mind, as if in a bubble above Claire's head: *He stayed with her for so long because she was good in bed.*

"I've consulted with a lawyer, and we've agreed that you may remain in the house if you like," Claire said, "and that Marina and I will find a new home. A fresh start for us seems essential. You can have her every other weekend, for one of the two major school vacations—we can alternate in alternate years—and for a month during the summer. I *do* want her to have access to you, Phil, and if some special occasion arises, I intend to be open and flexible. And in a half dozen years, say—when she's thirteen—I'd be agreeable to renegotiating the custody schedule. And yes, if she chooses to be Bat Mitzvah, I will encourage her in that choice. All right?"

"Flexibility sounds good. And access isn't bad," he replied. "But in terms of our evolutionary history, myth-making, you see—narrative, story-telling—preceded spoken words. I thought I should point that out. And theory—there's theory, of course. Theory's a latecomer to the whole process. Concepts such as flexibility and access, not to mention upfrontness—would have been unknown to our myth-making ancestors."

She sighed, and in her sigh he thought he heard a faint note of tenderness. "Oh Phil," she said, "will you snap out of it and face reality? The marriage is over. It has been for some time and I think we both knew it, though we've continued to go through the motions. I take full responsibility for my share of the failure, of course, and I want you to know that I do cherish the love we once had, and many of the good times. We brought a wonderful young woman into the world, and that young woman is at the center of my concern, as I hope she will be of yours."

"Oh sure. But listen, hey—which of the good times *didn't* you cherish? I'd be interested in knowing that."

"Stop it."

"I'm just seeking clarification. If I can understand your version of things, *your* story of our marriage—"

"Will you please just *stop* it? I don't want to—or have to—listen to this kind of verbal hair-splitting any longer. You still talk with me as if you're in one of your precious Talmud classes—as if you still resent me for somehow having stolen you from the world of your fathers."

"Hey," he said, raising his hands in a gesture of surrender. "How can we be direct without trading stories? When conquering rival societies, the first act of the conquerors is always to impose their myth—their version of reality, their *story*—on the conquered, so that if—"

"I'm warning you, Phil—"

"Now you'll insist we be *supportive* of one another, right?—that we respect one another's life-*styles*."

"You're mocking me again."

"Mimesis," he said. "Sure. How not, at a time like this? But in point of fact, the mimetic system remained functionally distinct from language, though it also came to reside, vestigially, within the phonological system, so that . . ."

"*Will you please just shut up!* Will you just shut up and talk to me like a human being, damn you!"

She was leaning toward him now, her face red.

He smiled, fully aware of just how insufferable he could be when he set his mind to the task.

"You're angry with me, aren't you?" he said.

"I really hate you when you get like this. I've tried to be civil—loving and caring—but you *are* nuts, Phil. And Marina knows it too, take my word for it. You're nuts the way your mother was nuts, and that goofy cousin of yours you always idolized so much. Milton what's-his-name—"

"*Martin*. Martin Landsberg."

"Martin then—the one who got locked away and jumped off—"

"Shh." He put a finger to his lips. "We shouldn't speak ill of the dead."

"You are *not* taking me seriously."

"I talk of death and evolution, mimesis and memory—the relation of myth to reality—and you say I'm not serious."

"You think you're smart, but you're just *word*-smart. You're still just that smart-aleck—" she hesitated, and in the brief silence he mouthed the word she did not utter—"*Jew*," "well, that smart-aleck know-it-all from Brooklyn, forever hiding behind jokes and sarcasm."

He saw no reason to counter anything she said—no reason, really, except for the small and momentary pleasure it might provide, to find flaws in her language or her logic. How many times had he said it to her through the years, that though he found a true argument about ideas, in which the parties brought real knowledge and passion to the table, exciting, he really never cared who won. It was the movement of mind that he loved, not mind's clever victories. What did you get, especially with someone you loved, if at the end of an argument one person won and one person lost? What *gain* that way?

He took a deep breath. "I'm sorry," he said softly.

"Good. Then this is what I think: I think we should tell Marina in the morning, and I think we should do so together. It's important that she understand we are divorcing from each other, and not from her."

Inside his mind—he could not, happily, locate the region with precision, though he suspected it might lie in the left hemisphere, near the inferior cerebral cortex—he saw himself wielding a large wet mop, and with this mop he was washing away all words and theory. When he saw that the task was completed, he leaned forward and spoke the words he now saw appear in his mind, one by one, like brightly colored play blocks upon a clean and gleaming marble floor.

"Marina-is-my-daughter-too," he said, "and-I-will-fight-you-to-the-death-for-her."

Claire's head snapped back. "What do you *mean?*"

"Mean?" he asked. "I mean what I said."

Claire got out of bed, put on her robe. "Don't come near me," she said. "Don't hit me."

"Hit you? Why would I hit you?"

"I'm going into Marina's room now. I'll sleep there tonight. You can have our bed."

"Oh Jesus," he said. "Cool it, okay? I'm pissed and frustrated and *very very* upset. Sure. But where the hell is all this coming from? Yesterday we were a happy family, or so I thought. And now—"

"I don't have to listen to you. I know what you get like when you lose your temper."

"Look, I haven't lost my temper for years. I don't *need* to lose my temper anymore, but if you need to believe you're married to a man who—"

"You're trying to confuse me with words again, but it won't work. I'm going into Marina's room, and I trust you'll respect our privacy. We'll give her the news in the morning."

"Just like that, right?"

She opened the door. He forced himself not to move toward her. "Look—leave Marina out of it, okay?" he said. "She's not your protector, for God's sake. You're-the-mother-she's-the-child, remember? Let's talk, then—let's really talk, instead of all this abracadabra and *mishegas* about lawyers. Come on. And why now? What did I do wrong *this* week? Why in heaven's name would you ever think I'd *hit* you?"

She shook her head. "You had your chance. I told you—I've been thinking about this for a long time—and last week, with the puppy, when I saw the way you struck it, I knew what I had to do."

"Good lord—*that* again? Sure I smacked it—lightly, firmly—to train it not to shit all over the house."

He heard barking, the patter of feet, a light rapping on their bedroom door.

"See?" she said. "Now you've done it—now you've woken them both."

"But note well," he said. "Our daughter always *knocks* before entering. As I've been trying to point out, the training of dogs and children has much in common."

Claire opened the door and Marina entered the room, thumb in mouth. Claire embraced her daughter, murmured lovingly in her ear. The puppy raced to Phil, started onto his lap, its tongue flapping away.

"*Down*," Phil said sharply, and the puppy stopped in its tracks, retreated, sat. Phil closed his eyes, heard the rest of their argument—saw the words unroll inside his head: How you couldn't housebreak a puppy simply by *loving* it—how tired he was of always being the disciplinarian, the bad cop, the ogre. The dog wanted and craved limits. And so did Marina. No child wanted to be more powerful than its parent. Marina couldn't be allowed, simply, to practice piano whenever she wanted, or watch TV whenever she wanted, or go to sleep whenever she wanted. When oh when was Claire going to take some responsibility—for the dog, for Marina, for the car, for their finances . . . ?

Across her mother's shoulder, Marina stared at him sleepily. "Is Daddy angry again?"

"Talk about training," he said.

"*Must* you?" Claire said. "What the child needs at a time like this is love, not sarcasm."

Claire kissed Marina's neck, then rose, took Marina by the hand, and walked from the room.

"Please," Phil said. "Please don't do this." The door closed. "It's not fair," he added.

The puppy—a three-month-old mutt, mostly terrier and black spaniel—licked Phil's hands. Phil scratched its head and ears, and when he did—when he felt its soft fur and flesh—he also felt tears well in his eyes.

"Shit," he said.

He walked from the bedroom, knocked on Marina's door.

"We don't *want* any," Marina called.

He opened the door, saw that Claire was lying under the covers, in bed with Marina.

"We would prefer to be left alone," Claire said.

"That's right," Marina said. "Mommies and daughters should be *alone* together."

He squeezed his eyes shut, then opened them, but his wife and daughter were still there. "Look," he said, "I'll sleep downstairs—whatever—but come back to our room now. Don't do this to her."

"I know you won't hurt me if I'm with her," Claire said.

"I'm begging you, okay?"

"We'll talk in the morning, when you've calmed down. I'm aware that my decision has come as a shock to you, but this is not the time to talk. Now please leave, so we can get some sleep."

"That's right," Marina said.

It was nearly midnight and, since most of the bars in downtown Amherst closed weeknights at eleven, he drove down from the hills of North Amherst, across Route 116, and out of town—into Hadley, a farming community where the population was mostly Polish. He drove past tobacco barns, open fields, houses set far apart from one another. Most of the houses were unlit, but here and there he saw a faint wash of color, luminescent and silver through drawn curtains, that he assumed came from television sets.

He listened to imaginary dialogues that took place inside his head—with Claire, with Marina, with lawyers, with therapists, with relatives, with friends—and decided that the scene he'd just been living in was one that was probably taking place, if with different words and in different styles, in tens of thousands of bedrooms all over America. Sure. More than half the children in Marina's elementary school were products of divorce: of blended families, joint custody schedules, single parenting, stepfathers, stepmothers, step-grandparents, family therapy, individual therapy, social workers, support groups . . . these were, simply, in this first decade of the twenty-first century in the United States of America, the arrangements that governed family life: the way people lived now.

Since he would, he figured, get little disagreement about the irresponsibility of Claire's action from others, what he had to wonder about, he knew, was his own responsibility in all this: about how and why he'd chosen Claire once upon a time, and how and why he'd stayed married to her, and, most of all, how and why he'd seen *none* of this coming.

He drove on, and found that the very darkness and silence—a world without spoken voices: the deserted road, the unlit homes, the dumb, glowing TV screens, the squared shapes of tobacco barns, long and firm against the flat land—gave his heart some ease. He turned north onto Route 47, toward Sunderland, where the road paralleled the gentle curves of the Connecticut River. In a few minutes, he saw the neon sign—*Kicza's*—pale and pink in the haze of low-lying clouds.

Inside, the large barn-like room was uncrowded, and the pleasant hum of voices, along with the music—Aretha Franklin, her voice uncharacteristically dim, as if muffled by the cigarette smoke, singing "Respect"—made him feel, strangely, at home. It was as if he had returned to one of the Irish bars that lined the streets of the Brooklyn neighborhood he'd known as a boy.

There were, he'd heard, wild goings-on here on weekends, when local rock bands performed, when potheads, townies, American

Legion types, bikers, and fraternity jocks sometimes went at one another and, so his students claimed—minor incidents transformed into myth?—wound up in pools of blood, emergency rooms, jails.

He took an empty seat at the bar, ordered a double Scotch, downed it in a single gulp, felt the heat flower inside his chest. He exhaled, as if—was it possible?—he had been holding his breath since he had left his house. Then he looked along the bar, and nodded to three men to his right. They acknowledged him politely, stared ahead with half-closed eyes and sullen expressions. From their dress and manner—bearded and scruffy, but in work clothes that seemed to have been used for work—he assumed they were locals: farmers, factory workers, part-time employees on the town's road crews.

The smoke was thick, and he took it in through his nostrils, enjoyed the way it cut into his sinuses; Amherst, where he lived, and the University of Massachusetts, where he taught, were both, by law, "smoke-free environments." He ordered another double Scotch, tilted his head back and downed it, the liquid rush sending streams of color cascading through his brain—he saw foaming, snow-capped waves roll in toward shore—then set the empty glass down, smiled, and ordered another.

He felt a hand on his shoulder, and, still smiling, he turned and looked into the familiar face of his favorite graduate student.

"So, Professor," Suzanne Cavelli said, "I have a question for you."

"Shoot—"

"What's a nice guy like you doing in a place like this?"

He grinned, gave Suzanne the old punch line: "Just lucky, I guess."

"No. Really. *Really*—" She rested a warm hand on his forearm. "I know it's none of my business, but are you all *right?* You look as if—well—as if you'd seen a ghost . . ."

They sat at a booth in the far corner of the room, drinking Scotch and trading stories. He told her about what had happened that evening and how surprised he had been (and how he was still in a state of bewilderment and shock)—and she told him about how her most recent boyfriend had taken her to lunch two weeks before to inform her, when dessert arrived, that he-had-met-somebody-else (and how, before the shock took hold, she had smiled sweetly, thanked him, and poured hot coffee onto his lap). She explained why she was there (she wasn't promiscuous, but she regarded flirting as a major indoor sport, and she found this place, in a word, *sexy*)—and he explained why he was there (he needed a drink in a place where, or so he'd thought, nobody would know his name).

He told her how worried he was about Marina (given the cruel bonding—the *folie à deux*—the mother was, at that very moment, inflicting upon the daughter)—and she told him about how worried she was that she might never have children (given her age—thirty-four—and successive break-ups of long-term relationships with men who seemed frightened of strong-willed women).

She told him about growing up in the Bronx (her mother and father owned a pizza parlor near Yankee Stadium)—and he told her about growing up in Brooklyn (his mother and father, observant Jews, owned a dry goods store not far from where Ebbets Field had once been). He told her that though he had until an hour or so before felt blessed to be living in a gorgeous, rural area of New England, he sometimes ached to be back in the city (to be riding the subways, to be pushing through crowds, to be surrounded by noise and dirt and the sounds of foreign languages)—and she told him she felt the same way (and that she had, three weeks before—no offense, since she found his classes a bright star in a sea of darkness—sent in transfer applications to doctoral programs at Columbia and NYU).

He told her how brilliant he'd always found her (and how this, more than her sultry, Italian beauty—which was real enough, he admitted—had made her so attractive to him)—and she told him how fascinating she'd always found him (and how it was the boyish passion with which he talked about things, more than his swarthy, Semitic good looks, which had fed her fantasy life).

She said that she wondered how much of her problem with men had to do with *her*—with her choices, and not with the men—and he said he had wondered how much of his problem with Claire had to do with *him*—with his choice, and not with Claire. He said that he had never, in the fourteen years since he'd met Claire, cheated on her (despite the passes many students and faculty wives sent his way)—and she said that she had always been true to her guys (despite the invitations sent her way). He said that he sometimes wondered, as now, if he had been so ferociously faithful merely because—good and driven Jewish boy that he still was—he somehow feared being *imperfect* (since, if you were imperfect, you were vulnerable)—and she said she sometimes wondered if she had always been so single-mindedly monogamous because—good and guilt-governed Catholic girl that she still was—she feared being rejected and abandoned (since, if you fell from grace through sin, you were bereft of God's love).

The bar closed. He looked around. How had she gotten there? Could he give her a ride home? She had come with a girlfriend, she said, but the friend had left.

"My intentions were strictly dishonorable," she said.

"Mine too," he said, then smiled. "At last," he added.

They sat in his car. She set her hand upon his thigh, and despite how drunk he was, he went hard at once. He kissed her, as gently as he could, his lips barely grazing hers.

Later they traded more stories and, after telling him about her parents' pizza parlor, and how she had, as a girl, known many of the Yankee players—Joe Pepitone, Reggie Jackson, others—and after he told her about eating garlic-and-mushroom pizzas at Luigi's in Brooklyn after Friday night basketball games, she asked him (referring, he assumed, to pizza) if he knew what the very best combination in the world was. He said that he did not.

"What's the very best combination in the world?" he asked.

"A Jewish boy and an Italian girl," she answered.

At dawn they drank champagne—she always kept a bottle on ice, she said, in expectation of an event worthy of celebration—and they agreed that, given the change in their status, things might become complicated.

"My problem," he said, "is that once I give my body, I always feel I have to throw my soul in too."

When he left—she rented two rooms in an old farmhouse in Conway, a village about ten miles northwest of Amherst—the sun was just rising in a clear autumn sky.

"You're an angel," he said.

She pressed her mouth gently to his neck, and told him that when it came to the relations of bodies to souls, their systems of belief were not dissimilar. Ever since he had praised her paper on Edelman's theories of neural Darwinism, she had sensed that it was so, she said. He laughed, after which she assured him that everything was going to be all right because if it was true that she was an angel—and why shouldn't she believe him?—then in the hierarchy of such beings—in hosts of heavenly ghosts—her rank was surely that of *guardian* angel.

Still, she added, she worried more about Marina than about him. In his mind's eye, he saw Marina in the open window of her second-story bedroom. She was wearing her ballet costume, toy-store angel wings strapped to her back, and she was declaring that unless he and Claire promised to stay together forever, she was going to jump out the window and fly away.

Would he call her later in the day? Suzanne asked. On the porch, her warm body set against the curve of his own, he wondered if scenes such as this were taking place at that moment on thousands of porches all across America.

"I'll want you again, you know," she said. She kissed him lovingly on the cheek, lifted his hand, kissed his palm, pushed him away from her, toward his car, then spoke: "When I go back inside, I'm going to pray for you, as well as for Claire and Marina."

Briefly, he imagined introducing Claire to Suzanne, saw them shaking hands. Seeing them together, in silhouette, he saw, too, just how predictable his couplings had been: the poor, bright, intense Jewish boy—and the wealthy, genteel, demure Gentile girl; the brilliant, unhappy, aging professor—and the mature, lonely, adoring graduate student.

He blinked, walked to his car, got in, turned the key in the ignition, and drove off, all the while picturing Claire and Suzanne, in his home, walking upstairs together. They undressed, got into bed, and invited him to join them. Surely, he assured himself, it was easier to imagine this than to imagine what actually lay in wait for him—not the legal stuff and custody battles so much, he realized, as the words—as all the goddamned *words* he was going to have to listen to, from Claire and lawyers and friends and relatives and social workers and therapists and who-knew-who-else.

Worst of all, though, he knew, were the words that were going to rise from his own throat. Sure. That had, of course, been the major turning point in evolution—when the larynx had changed ever so slightly—and had, thereby, separated *Homo sapiens* from the primates. Our enlarged brain size alone, without the ability to speak—without the change in the curvature of the major articulatory muscles of the pharynx, itself a result, probably, of the change in curvature of the basal surface of the skull—this, rather than bipedalism, seemed to him the most significant event in the relation of evolution to consciousness; for without language, of what use the changes in brain size or intellectual capacity? Our brain, if larger, remained typically primate; our vocal apparatus did not.

Very small changes led eventually to large issues, whether through the course of millions of years of evolution, or through the evolution of a single marriage, or the events of a single night, or a single moment. The perceptual and motor devices that made speech possible (the length and angle of the Neanderthal neck, for example, could never have accommodated the human vocal apparatus), thus, had probably evolved as a single, radical adaptation. And from this fact . . .

He imagined Suzanne raising her hand, but he could imagine her face only, and so could not tell if she were raising her hand in a classroom or in a bedroom. He thought of talking with her about this—about how the mind saw things, though it did not know exactly what it was *seeing*. How, after all, could a mind, without eyes, *see?* This was still the great mystery and wonder to him—that the Suzanne he saw in his mind, even as he stared ahead and saw, simultaneously, a road and trees (and saw, too, Claire, Marina, the dog, his desk lamp, his desk, a page on the desk, footnotes at the bottom of the page, a reference in need of correction)—was not the Suzanne he had ever seen at any particular moment in time. Memory was, as ever, creation. Of course, he heard Suzanne say, but wouldn't he agree with her, too, that the debate over the origin of language was really a debate about the emergence of all uniquely *human* styles of representation?

The lights were on in his kitchen. It was not yet 7:30, which meant that, responsible as ever, he had managed to arrive home in time to see Marina off to school. He entered the kitchen, smiled at his wife and daughter, who sat across from each other at the dining room table, kissed each of them on the forehead, and when he did—sweet surprise—Marina smiled up at him and kissed him back.

The Imported Man

Isaac Klein, a retired piece goods finisher living in West Palm Beach, Florida, walked through the aisles of Stein's Department Store and found that he was, as always, comforted by the noise. Even before his wife Sylvia had died, fourteen months before, leaving him alone in their two-room garden apartment in Crestwood Village, he had enjoyed accompanying her to Stein's, though he had not realized then that it was the sound—the high, constant volume of noise—that had pleased him. Now, however, as he rode the escalator from the second to the first floor, he knew that he made the daily half-mile journey from his apartment to the shopping plaza expressly to stroll through the wonderful sounds—bells, cash registers, music, voices—for it was when he was lost in these sounds that he could most easily imagine that he was Franzl Nassofer, the Minnesota Vikings' new Austrian place-kicking specialist.

Nassofer came from Nikitsch, a small village in eastern Austria, near the Hungarian border and less than twenty miles from Zsira, the Hungarian village in which Isaac had been born. Football itself did not interest Isaac. He had only begun watching games at his wife's suggestion so that he might have something to talk about with other men. But if the game meant little to him, what, he wondered again, as he had the first time he discovered that foreigners played for American teams, could it mean to an imported man who understood neither the language nor the rules?

He was halfway down the escalator when he saw the woman's eyes.

They were fixed upon his own, and they appeared hurt and startled. Wedged between several shoppers—his eyes followed the movement of her eyes downward—she was stuffing something into her purse.

Isaac left the store and walked along the sidewalk. There were three rows of benches in front of Merrill Lynch's Crestwood Village office, and elderly men sat on them, staring at windows in which computerized light bulbs passed the results of the day's trading in New York. Isaac sat in the second row, among his friends. They asked him who he liked in the Monday night game of the week, and he picked the Dallas Cowboys over the New York Jets. (The Cowboys had a kicker from Vienna named Fritsch; the Jets' man, Howfield, came from England.) The other men nodded, and Isaac felt pleased.

He listened as the men traded stories concerning friends and relatives they had left behind in Brooklyn, the Bronx, Queens, Newark. Like their wives, Isaac noticed, they seemed most excited when they spoke of how lucky they were to have left—when they blessed their new lives by sharing reports from the North: of muggings and rapes, theft and filth. But what will there be there for me to do every day? he had asked Sylvia before they left Brooklyn, and she had answered that a man who had worked as hard as he had, for over fifty years, was entitled to retire: to rest, to swim, to lie in the sun, to find new interests, to enjoy himself.

He left the shopping plaza, crossed the wooden bridge that joined it to Crestwood Village, and saw, in the distance, the series of low two-story buildings that contained his apartment. Beyond the apartments lay the rolling hills of one of the village's two eighteen-hole golf courses. Remembering, as a boy, walking across the Brooklyn Bridge in the middle of winter, a bucket of coal in each hand in order to save twelve cents, Isaac concluded that there really had been no way to deny Sylvia's reply to his question.

The following Sunday afternoon, he was alone in his bedroom when he heard a knock at the door. Near the end of the second quarter, the New York Giants were losing to the Detroit Lions 10 to 0, and Gogolak, their Hungarian placekicker (he had a brother who kicked for the New England Patriots), had not yet had a chance to score. He went to the front door.

"Hello," the woman said. "I'm Shirley Mandel, one of your neighbors here in Crestwood, and I'd like to tell you about our physical fitness club, Mister Klein." She spoke mechanically. Isaac heard the crowd's roar, from the bedroom. "Keeping in shape is a way of life for many Crestwood residents, you know."

"What?" he asked, and he looked at her for the first time.

"Keeping in shape is a way of life for many Crestwood residents," she replied. "The truth is, we women decided to go out this afternoon because we know how many of you men are watching your football games. We—"

"You interrupted me," Isaac said, squinting in order to see her better.

"I knew Sylvia," she said.

"I'm sorry," he said. "I'm not interested."

He closed the door and saw that his hands were trembling. He sat on the bed and realized that he had missed the score of the Minnesota game. He rested his head on pillows and watched the twenty-two players charge toward one another. *Keeping in shape is a way of life.* What, he wondered, could such a statement mean?

Isaac had arrived in America with his father and older brother in 1912, when he was eleven years old; before he had been in the country a week they began working in a factory owned by a cousin, pairing socks and putting them in wrappers. His mother and younger brother arrived in 1914, sent for with the money the three of them earned. When he was twenty years old, a piece goods finisher in a factory on West 38th Street, he had fallen in love with a girl from the factory, with whom he had never spoken. Her name was Esther Plaut, and he gave this name to his father. Two months later his father told him that a marriage was arranged between Isaac and Sylvia, Esther's older sister. Sylvia's father could not marry off the younger sister until the older one was settled. Isaac visited the Plaut apartment with his father, and saw no way to object to the arrangement. According to the agreement between the fathers, Sylvia was never to know of Isaac's original wish, and Isaac had, until her death, honored the agreement.

When had he had time for friends? He left their apartment in Brooklyn at 7:30 each morning, riding the IRT to Manhattan. For forty-eight years, beginning seventeen months before his marriage, he worked for Distinctive Apparel. When there was no overtime he returned home at 6:30 each evening. He ate his supper, and listened to Sylvia tell him how she had spent the day. Then he read his newspaper, and by ten o'clock he went to sleep. If he had had children, he wondered, would his life have been different? Would he have had friends then? He had never, in truth, liked children—their eyes, forever hungry, he thought, made him nervous—but it was possible, he granted, that he might have liked children of his own.

He watched the videotaped replay of a tall player leaping high in the air, between defenders, to catch a pass. The announcer talked of other games. In Minnesota, he said, a rookie from Austria named Franzl Nassofer had kicked a twenty-seven-yard field goal in the closing minutes of the first half to put the Vikings ahead of the Redskins, 13 to 10.

Isaac sighed and closed his eyes. What, as Nassofer ran off the field, with Viking fans yelling at him, was he feeling? As he sat in the locker room, sucking an orange, of what was he thinking? Had he been frightened when he saw the men charging at him? Isaac thought of his own hands, trembling when Mrs. Mandel left. In his head, as he watched Giants and Lions grapple with one another, Isaac practiced dialogues, in Hungarian, German, and Yiddish. Was it possible—no mention of it had ever been made—that, with a name like Nassofer, he was also Jewish?

Isaac rested on pillows, his head back, watching the game between the posts of his socked feet. He felt warm. He was glad he had had the will to refuse the invitations of the other men to watch the games with them. Stenerud, Yepremian, the Gogolaks, Howfield, Walker, Herrera, Fritsch, Muhlmann, Nassofer—he wondered if they got together with one another in the off-season, or if they had been able to become friends with members of their own teams. Did they receive invitations to receptions at the embassies of the nations from which they had come? Did local Hungarian-American and Austrian-American clubs give them dinners? Since they had to learn only one play, to be used one day a week for fourteen weeks (plus exhibitions and play-offs), what did they do with all their free time? How did they use their money? Did any of them plan to return to their native lands?

Isaac thought of writing to Nassofer, of taking the boy to dinner when the Vikings came to Miami. He could, if they met, ask Nassofer such questions. First, of course, he would inquire about the boy's family—he would find out if there were things that, as one who had been in America for more than sixty years, he could do for him.

On the television screen the game moved slowly, along the ground. Isaac tried to think of ways in which he might help Nassofer, and then, as if the picture tube had exploded before his eyes, he was shaken from his dreams. *What if Nassofer did not make the team?* What if, when the season began, they cut him and sent him back to Nikitsch? Isaac imagined himself, as a young man, returning to Zsira, his pockets empty. What banquets and wishes must have been given to Nassofer before he left for the New World! How his soccer teammates, left behind, must now talk about him! If he were cut from the team, yet decided to stay in the United States to wait for another season in order to try again, could he get a job? Was he trained in anything? What, Isaac wondered, would he do with his time for a year, and with whom?

Early Monday morning Isaac walked to the shopping plaza and bought a copy of the *Miami Herald*. He sat on one of the empty benches in front of the Merrill Lynch office and turned to the sports pages: Nassofer had kicked one field goal and one extra point. Isaac left the newspaper on the bench. He wanted to be gone before his friends arrived. What excited them were rifle-armed quarterbacks and dazzling broken-field runners.

He reached the end of the shopping plaza. To his left, from the direction of the clubhouse, he saw a pack of villagers in bright red sweatshirts, jogging. He moved quickly, so as not to be caught by them. If he was different from the others, he wondered, where had this difference come from? When was it, he asked himself, that he had ever had time to take in things that now allowed him to be different? He did not recall being a man who had ever agreed or disagreed with others about anything.

He walked swiftly across the sidewalks of Crestwood Village. He passed empty benches and did not look at the goldfish in the wading pools. He wanted very much to find that point in his own life that had led to the moment in which he was now living. His willingness to imagine himself as Nassofer, he decided, could not have come from nowhere.

In front of the door to his apartment lay a small package wrapped in glistening blue and silver paper and tied with a white ribbon. He picked it up and entered the apartment. He opened the package and found a new cocoa-colored wallet inside. He saw the woman's eyes again, hurt and startled. He turned on an electric burner and boiled water. He nodded to himself, and felt his heart constrict: the night of his marriage, he recalled, over fifty-one years before, when he and Sylvia were alone, and when he closed his eyes, he had made himself imagine that he was with Sylvia's sister Esther.

There it was, he sighed, and he put a spoonful of instant coffee into a cup. Still, if he had done such a terrible thing—so terrible that he had forced himself to forget until this moment that it had happened—how was it that something good could have come from it? He sat at the kitchen table, the wallet beside the saucer, and sipped his coffee. He wondered if the man named Dempsey, who kicked for the Philadelphia Eagles, a man who had a stump for an arm and a short piece of wood for a foot (a half-foot, which he wore inside a special square-toed football shoe), had, because of his physical shape, a special affinity with the imported kickers. Dempsey held the all-time record for the longest field goal—sixty-three yards.

The telephone rang and Isaac answered it. "Hello," a woman said. "This is Shirley Mandel—you'll forgive me for calling, Mr. Klein, but I wanted to apologize for interrupting you yesterday. There's another game tonight, and I thought if you were free you might like to come to my apartment to watch it." He was surprised at the steadiness of her voice. "We could have some coffee and cake, and I could invite some others if you like."

"I'm sorry," he said.

She laughed. "When Sylvia died I thought often of doing something for you, but I was held back by . . ." Isaac waited, but said nothing. "Are you certain you won't come?"

"Yes," Isaac said.

"Well, thank you," she said. "Maybe another time, now that we know one another. I'm a widow, you're a widower, why should we stand on ceremonies?" Her voice was direct and easy, but he did not believe she would have said such things if she were in his presence. "Why should we ask so much of life, at our age? Enjoy your game, Isaac."

She hung up. Isaac stuffed the wrapping paper from the wallet into a wastebasket, below the sink. He left the wallet on the table, not wanting to touch it, or to make a decision as to whether he would or would not use it. He left the apartment. In front of the Merrill Lynch office his friends were already gathered, discussing the previous day's games.

He said the Giants had looked bad. "But I like Nassofer," he said.

"Who?"

"Nassofer—the new placekicker for the Vikings."

When they lived in New York, one man said, the Giants were champions—now that they lived here, the Dolphins were champions.

"God favors the Jews," Isaac said, and the men laughed. One of them patted him on the back, with affection. "The Vikings will be on television next Monday night," he added. "Watch out for Nassofer."

During the week, his routine remained the same. He rose early, walked to the shopping plaza for his newspaper, returned home for breakfast. He cleaned his apartment, then left again and walked through Stein's. He sat on benches and talked with his friends, but he did not mention Nassofer again, and nobody mentioned Nassofer to him.

After lunch, he napped, the telephone receiver off the hook—a luxury he allowed himself now that he was living alone; he had been impressed, many years before, when he had telephoned the husband of one of Sylvia's friends after lunch one afternoon, only to be told by the man's wife, "My husband is taking his nap—can you call back later?"

In the afternoons he swam at the village's clubhouse or strolled on the golf course near his building. In the evenings he watched television—whatever was on—while he worked, in his head, on a letter to Nassofer. The regular season would begin in two weeks—should he write to Nassofer before then, in case the boy was dropped from the team? Or would suggesting the possibility to him in some way, as sports people put it, *jinx* him?

He tried to concentrate on what he might suggest should Nassofer be cut from the team. He wondered if he himself would have wanted to return to the other side, or if he would have tried to stay on in America, and he found no answer. What he desired—the only thing, really—was, as often as possible, to be able to run onto the playing field, to kick the ball as far and as accurately as he could, and to hear the thundering ovation of strangers. Without that, in truth, he could see no good reason to go on.

He feared then, he realized, for Nassofer's life, and he tried to think of words he might use to let the boy know that he was not alone. And then—it happened on Saturday afternoon, when Stein's was more crowded than usual—he saw how silly his fears were. He realized, with an abrupt and definite movement of his heart downward, that he had never before considered the difference: between being Nassofer and imagining that he was Nassofer.

He turned away at once. He bumped into several women, but, without apologies, pushed toward the escalator. The question seemed too difficult, coming so late. The game was only two days away, and—yes!—there was a difference between being on the field and being the man who was kicking the ball, and being a man who *imagined* that he was on the field and was kicking the ball, though Isaac did not see how he would ever be able to know what that difference was.

"Are you all right?"

He moved away from the voice, toward the front door. If Nassofer could have imagined that he was Isaac Klein, and if he then could imagine what Isaac Klein imagined . . .

"Your color is terrible, Isaac. You should get some air."

She held his arm and led him from the store. Her shopping bag rustled against his hip.

"Why?" he asked, not bothering to look into her eyes.

She sighed. "Why," she repeated.

His question had not been directed to her, but he saw no reason to tell her that. He pulled away and began walking along the sidewalk, toward the other end of the shopping plaza.

He did not leave his apartment for the next two days. He prepared his meals, he rested, he looked out his living room window at the other apartments, at the hills and palm trees and the golf course, and he waited for the game. The question remained, but he was not, he knew, prepared to deal with it. He had had nothing in his life, he told himself, that had prepared him to answer it.

On Monday night, in the first period against the Oakland Raiders, Cox, the regular Minnesota field goal kicker, kicked an extra point. The

Raiders scored a touchdown and a field goal early in the second quarter, and added another field goal in the last minutes. The half ended and Nassofer had not played. The Vikings trailed 13 to 7.

Nassofer opened the second half by kicking off, and the announcer—Isaac was certain he heard him—mentioned the village in Austria from which he had come, and the fact that he was one of the rookies the Viking coaches wanted to have a last look at before final cuts were made. The kickoff was taken at the Raider twelve yard line—not, Isaac knew, a strong effort.

The game moved along, and Isaac followed it attentively. There was no point in wondering about what, on the sidelines, Nassofer was thinking, though Isaac had not, he assured himself, forsaken the boy.

Late in the fourth quarter, the Vikings trailed 16 to 14. With a minute and twelve seconds left, their quarterback engineered a drive from their own sixteen yard line to the Raider thirty-seven. Isaac's heart pounded. With six seconds left on the clock and the crowd roaring, Nassofer prepared to trot out onto the field, his left arm held momentarily by a Viking coach. Isaac did not have time to think. Before he knew it the teams had lined up, Nassofer had run out, had snapped his chin strap to his helmet, had paced off the necessary steps, the ball had been hiked, the quarterback had set it down, the crowd's roar had peaked, Nassofer had run forward at an angle, had spread his arms sideways for balance—as if he were a boy making believe he was an airplane—and had kicked. The ball, traveling low—as, the announcer pointed out, soccer-style kicks often did—never passed beyond the line of scrimmage. It was deflected by a defensive lineman and skittered along the ground. Nassofer kicked at the ground, players fell on the ball, the game was over.

Isaac sighed. He watched the play again, in a slow-motion videotaped replay, but he saw nothing he had not already seen. He left the television on, in case there was an interview—though why should it be with Nassofer?—and he walked in his socked feet to the kitchen, to get some water. He answered the phone.

"I'm sorry," Shirley said.

"It's all right," Isaac replied.

"I've been thinking about it—why—since last week. Please don't be upset by what I do, Isaac. I'd like to stop. Believe me."

He agreed to meet her, the next morning, for coffee and cake. Then he climbed back onto his bed and stared at the television screen. They were not interviewing Nassofer. Maybe, he thought, Nassofer owned a sports car he had bought with the bonus money the Vikings paid him. Isaac closed his eyes and let his head sink into his two pillows, which were stacked against the headboard. Many of the young players—and who could blame them?—spent the money almost before they earned it: on clothes, women, cars. That was America too, Isaac knew.

Isaac imagined the coach giving Nassofer the bad news, telling him to come back the following year, to try to hook up with a semi-pro team in the interim. He watched Nassofer walk from the office, and from the stadium. He saw him step into his little red sports car, turn on the ignition, and gun the engine. Was it fair, Isaac asked, that this should have happened after such a journey? The car's tires squealed as it shot from the curb. Soon it was on the highway and Isaac felt anger rising within him. There were so many questions! If he could calm down, he knew, he would have been able to ask them forever, though none of them would have helped. He felt so much for Nassofer—so much!—yet how could he do anything now that he knew there was such a difference? Everything had to be rethought, and there was no time.

Isaac pressed a button on his remote control switch so that light and sound vanished from the television screen. He listened to the sound of his own breathing, and he felt more angry, more passionate, more helpless than ever. He could, he knew, have watched the speedometer inside Nassofer's car pass 80, 90, or 100. He could have visualized the curve, the wet spot on the highway—but what for? If he let himself speculate in this way, if he began to let his head fill up with things about which he could never be certain, how would he ever stop? The wisest thing, he decided, his heart breaking, was to forget Nassofer. He hoped the boy would understand that a man who had worked as hard as he had, for over fifty years, was entitled to retire: to rest, to swim, to lie in the sun, to find new interests, to enjoy himself.

Have You Visited Israel?

She made her way back along Broadway, scanning the sidewalk for the wallet she feared she would not find. At 110th Street she stopped, opened her mouth, let a snowflake melt on her tongue, then pressed her eyes closed and imagined she was alone at four a.m. on the Pont Neuf, the first woman in Paris to know that it was snowing.

She entered the cafeteria, went to the table where she had sat an hour earlier. The wallet was not there. She went to the cashier and asked if anybody had turned in a wallet. The woman said no.

The young man who had been sitting at the table next to hers was still there, drinking coffee and reading the *New York Times*.

"Excuse me," she said, "but I saw you here awhile ago. I seem to have lost my wallet—I had it when I was here, and then when I got to where I was going, it was gone."

He smiled. "I will make inquiries," he said. "Yes. Please tell me your name."

"Ruth. Ruth Rabinowitz."

"And where are you from, Ruth Rabinowitz?"

"Shaker Heights," she said. "It's in Ohio—a suburb of Cleveland. But I'm here now." She laughed. "Of course I'm here. What I mean to say is, I go to school near here—to Barnard."

"Rabinowitz is originally Rebbe Novitch," he said. "Did you know that? You are then Russian and Jewish, like myself. I am also Israeli, so we have made most different journeys since once upon a time in Russia. But I am here now as student, too, at Columbia, studying physics.

My name is Aharon Mirsky."

He extended a hand and she shook it.

"Would you join me for coffee or tea?"

She hesitated. "Thank you, but I need to find my wallet or else . . ." She paused. "I'm just very upset and—yes—all right. I'm sorry. Tea, please. Thank you."

When he walked to the counter she saw that he had no left hand. Where the hand would have been, there was a stump covered with a black sock.

He returned and she sipped her tea, holding the cup with both hands for warmth.

"I will put you at ease," Aharon said. He smiled, gestured to his missing hand. "The cause: merely border raid that enabled me to leave from front lines to hospital and then to Army intelligence and then back to university in Haifa and then to university in America. A small loss, really, that may have provided me with long and happy life. I was not born to be hero."

"I'm sorry. I hope I wasn't staring."

"Not yet."

She laughed. "I'm sorry."

"You have said that three times already."

"But who's counting?" she said, and then: "I'm sorry."

They laughed together.

"Children stare," he said, "but adults *sneak* looks because they are ashamed of interest. I was merely random victim of, for us, ordinary event. I killed two Arabs and prevented them from blowing up their destination—school attended by children to age of twelve. The two Arabs were themselves boys of thirteen, although official reports said they were nineteen. Have you visited Israel?"

"No."

"Did you have important credentials or money in wallet, for I see you have purse with you still."

"I don't know." She felt tears well in her eyes. "I can replace other things, I suppose—but yes, there was money."

"So. Talk to me, Ruth Rabinowitz. If you had wallet in purse, somebody might have taken it, removed money and, as is the custom here, put into postal box for return. It would give me pleasure to be your friend today. Will you allow to do that for me? I am stranger in strange land, yes? Please tell me story of what happened."

She took a deep breath and found herself telling him about Kevin. Kevin had graduated from Columbia College the year before and, on a fellowship in linguistics, was now studying at the Sorbonne. She and Kevin had known one another for eleven months, but being apart was proving harder than either of them had imagined it would be.

She and Kevin had talked about getting married, she explained, but Kevin said they should spend an extended period of time together before they made a decision—away from New York, away from their families, away from school. Kevin was not Jewish, she added, and her parents disapproved of him.

"And Kevin's family?"

"They're proud of him and they accept me. They're Irish Catholics, from Albany. His father is an accountant, his mother a housewife—they're very traditional, and I really like them. Kevin is the eldest of seven children—he has four sisters and two brothers. And, oh yes, his parents hoped he would become a priest, which seems standard operating procedure for the eldest boy in a family like his."

She laughed.

"Yes?"

"There are times when I think they may yet get their wish. Kevin is very *moral*, you see." She smiled. "In the Olympics of guilt, I said to him once—after we'd spent a weekend at his parents' home—compared to the Catholics, I think the Jews would get a bronze."

She stopped. "But tell me: why am I mouthing off to you like this?" she asked, and then answered her own question: "Because I am extremely anxious even though I *seem* calm. But I had four hundred dollars cash in my wallet. If I don't pay today, I'll lose my reservations—it was one of those special flights where you pay for the ticket within twenty-four hours and if you cancel there's no refund. I mean, even if I find the money, tomorrow, or the day after . . . ?"

What she was imagining as she looked into Aharon's eyes, she realized, was how her parents might receive the news: that she had met somebody else, a young Israeli who was studying to be a doctor—of physics, not medicine—but a doctor nonetheless; of how she was going to help him through graduate school while they had their first child; of how, once he had received his doctorate, he would support her and the child, at which time she would complete her education . . .

"I will help you, Ruth Rabinowitz. I was in intelligence, yes? And you are wonderful and most attractive young woman."

"How do you know?"

"Ah," he said. "How do I know." He smiled. His right front tooth was chipped, like a large apostrophe, she thought—like the Hebrew letter "yud"—and she wanted to tell him that his two front teeth made her think of the letters for the word "chai": the letters that, since numbers and letters were the same in Hebrew, formed the number eighteen as well as the word for life. She imagined putting a note between stones in the Wailing Wall, wedging the note in as far as she could. But what, besides finding the money, would she wish for? What, after all, did she truly *desire*? She felt tears well in her eyes.

Aharon reached across and, with his good hand, took her hand in his own. "First," he said, "you must telephone Kevin and explain what happened."

He told her what numbers to press. He was surprised that she did not know how to do such a thing. He thought all American college students knew how to deceive telephone and credit card companies. He said he would prepare tea for them. So that she might have privacy, he went into the alcove that was his kitchen, and drew a curtain closed behind him.

"Did I wake you?"

"What—? No. I had to get up to answer the phone anyway."

"This is Ruth."

"I know. This is Kevin. Look. I'll see you in less than a week. Sweet dreams."

"No, don't go away. You're not awake yet, but listen to me. I love you. But we ran into some difficulties—I did—and I wanted you to know right away."

"What happened?"

She explained, and when she finished her story, Kevin did not speak. She imagined herself on a bridge in Paris, Kevin walking away from her, disappearing in the snow.

"I miss you," she said. "I love you and I miss you."

"Then why did you lose the money?"

"It was an accident."

"There are no accidents."

"Oh Kevin. Please?"

"How could you lose all that cash, and why were you carrying it around? Why didn't you get a cashier's check from the bank?"

"Because I took out your letter when I stopped for breakfast, to read it for the fourth or fifth time. Because . . . I don't *know*! Maybe I left my purse open then. But I'm sorry and can't you understand how upset I am about this, about our plans?" She lowered her voice, whispered: "I just miss you so much sometimes it hurts *physically* . . ."

"And it hurt so much that you got careless again."

"*Again?*"

"You have never been to the Negev," Aharon said, handing her a cup of tea. "Let me, then, to tell you about myself. I am twenty-eight years old and married. I have two children, a girl and boy—the choice of kings, as we say. The boy is six, the girl four. But wife and I have not slept together for nearly two years. Still, we concluded an agreement before departure: that if either of us meets someone else, then we will give to the other freedom. Otherwise there is no reason. But there is also this: we loved one another enough once to marry and bear children and so we will wait to see how life travels and perhaps our love will bloom again. Do you know about desert flowers, and how they may not bloom for one or many years and then they do?"

When she told him about her conversation with Kevin, he did not comment. Instead he told her that she had beautiful Russian eyes—deep brown, almost black, like his own—and that he had noticed her in the cafeteria that morning because she had seemed very happy. "There are few things in life," he said, "as miraculous as beautiful woman when she is happy."

"That was when I had four hundred dollars," she laughed. "That was when I was filled with the prospect of three weeks in Paris with my lover."

She had never called Kevin her lover before, and it made her feel very grown-up to do so. She closed her eyes briefly, and when she opened them, Aharon touched her cheek gently, with his good hand. Then he kissed her.

He took her hand and led her to his couch. They sat, and he kissed her again. She opened her mouth to him, put her hands on the back of his neck, then closed her eyes and imagined snow swirling in gusts, rising, fading into air. She lay back, and felt a desire to be so small that she would be able to crawl inside his mouth, where she would be lost forever.

His hand was under her sweater, resting gently on her stomach, she realized a while later, though she had no idea as to how much time had passed. She smiled while he nibbled at her left ear. Oh God, she thought. I am going straight to heaven. I will not pass "GO." I will not collect four hundred dollars. Snow filled her head, sifted down, tumbling through her, warming her, and, after a while, she lost all sense of how long she had been gazing at the white flakes, or how long it was since Aharon had removed the sock and was inside her with his stump.

When she awoke, he was gone. On the table next to the bed she saw her wallet, and a note. The note said that she was a wonderful woman and that he had taken advantage only so that they could come to know one another. He was not truly a thief—except that had he intended, yes, to steal her heart. Was he too bold? If so, he hoped she would forgive him. Might she stay in the apartment if she wished, or return at 6:45 in the evening for a quiet dinner? He remained her good friend, Aharon Mirsky.

She closed her eyes, luxuriated in the soreness she was feeling below. She did not want to put on her clothes, or to bathe. It was enough to lie where she was, far from home, where nobody she knew could find her. She reread Aharon's note. She liked the graceful, somewhat feminine curve of his handwriting, and wondered if the hand he used now was the one he had first used to write with when he was a schoolboy. She imagined herself sliding along the lines of his script as if they were heat waves vibrating in hot air above desert sands. She opened her wallet and counted the money, then placed the money back inside the wallet, and the wallet back inside her purse.

Stairs

Sarah Miller arrives home after a two-and-a-half-hour trip—a bus and two trains—with a list inside her head of the things her son Carl wants her to bring him the next visiting day: Cuban cigars, life insurance policies, a compass, a model airplane kit, sucking candies, a deck of pinochle playing cards, old photos from summer camp. Outside her apartment building, Mr. Barton, the elderly black superintendent, shows her a picture from the *New York Post* of an open locker and a blanket—the custodian of Walt Whitman Junior High School has found a dead baby in the girls' locker room. Sarah Miller stares at the picture—a bundle on the floor in front of a locker—but she cannot see the baby.

Carl had graduated from Walt Whitman Junior High twenty-nine years before. He was elected treasurer of the school's general organization, and she wonders for a moment why nobody warned her, through the years, of what was to come. One day he was a normal boy, an engineering student in his second year at the City College of New York, and the next day he was tied into a straitjacket, his tongue swollen to double its size. Sarah Miller bites down lightly on her own tongue. Sometimes, alone in her apartment, she bites harder, to feel what she imagines Carl must have felt. But even when she blots her tongue and examines the pinpoints of blood on her handkerchief, she cannot understand how he was able to do it.

Mr. Barton tells her that the dead baby weighed less than three pounds. Sarah Miller imagines that Carl is in the photo, hiding under the blanket. Listen, she wants to say. What makes sense? A black baby rots in a rusty locker while my son Carl goes stiff like a frozen bird.

She sees Carl's eyes close as his mouth opens. She calls an aide and he calls another, and when Carl's arms go straight and his knees move up and lock, the aides carry him off and tie him into his bed.

"How's your Carl feeling these days?" Mr. Barton asks.

"The same."

"I always liked Carl," Mr. Barton says.

Sarah Miller enters the building, which smells strongly of Lysol and ammonia. She appreciates the fact that Mr. Barton works hard to keep the building clean. The wooden banisters shine, the marble stairs glisten.

Often, as now, when she looks up the stairs, she remembers her father falling down. "*Poppa!*" she wanted to cry out. "*Oh, Poppa!*" Her mother stood at the top of the stairs, arms folded across her chest, screaming at him. Sarah Miller held her schoolbooks to her chest and watched her father get up and wipe himself off. He smiled at her, blood on his forehead. She was afraid to move, yet there seemed to be something very natural and ordinary about what was happening. "*You leave her alone!*" her mother screamed. "*You leave her alone! When you can feed her, then she'll be your daughter!*" Sarah Miller remembers that she wanted to wipe away blood from her father's forehead, but that instead she stayed where she was while her father stumbled past her, out and into the street.

Sarah Miller starts up the stairs. After visits to Carl, she often finds herself seeing scenes in her head, from childhood. She stopped bringing friends home because of how fiercely her parents fought. Would the police be there? That was her great fear—that the neighbors would call the police and the police would be waiting, as they sometimes were, in the kitchen.

"*Momma threw Poppa down the stairs. Did you see?*" Her older sister, Rosalind, would puff up her chest and cross her arms above her breasts, as if *she* were their mother. "*Momma threw Poppa down the stairs.*"

Years later, after Sarah Miller left home and married Arnold, her father came to her apartment from his old-age home. She served him a hot meal, and when her mother discovered what she had done, she told Sarah she would never speak to her again.

She kept her word. Ah, the world of our fathers, Sarah Miller thinks, then smiles, for in their family, their *mother* was the one who took care of the building, who fixed the furnace, repaired broken windows, cemented the sidewalk, and collected the rent. The money to purchase the building came from her mother's father, who had been a cattle dealer in New Jersey. Sarah Miller remembers coming home from school in winter, turning the corner with her friend Lena, and seeing her mother on her knees, bent over in front of their door, chopping at the sidewalk with a hammer. "What's your mother *doing?*" Lena asked. Too embarrassed to answer, Sarah Miller had run past her mother and up the stairs.

Sarah Miller stops at each landing to catch her breath. She remembers listening to her father, years after her mother had died, telling her that he had loved her mother so much he had not known what to do when she turned on him. Before they were married, she had been proud of his brilliance and his knowledge—but later, when he had spent his days wandering from *shul* to *shul* and house to house, teaching young boys to read, and training them for their Bar Mitzvahs, she had mocked him. "*A* melamed *I married!*" she would cry. "*A melamed. One who cannot even tie a cat's tail becomes a* melamed! *If you loved me, you would stop!*"

Sarah Miller unlocks her door, takes off her coat and scarf. She makes herself a glass of tea and puts a spoonful of strawberry jam in it, the way her father did. Momma threw Poppa down the stairs, she says to herself, but who threw Carl down? And why does he break all the time? She sits by the kitchen window and looks out through the bars of the fire escape. At the corner a man is stuffing his garbage into a mailbox.

She remembers when Carl slept on the fire escape with his cousin Herbie, who is now an electrical engineer for IBM in Ossining, New York. They used to play together, hour after hour, at their erector sets and chemistry sets, their chess games and card games. Sarah Miller is grateful that Arnold is gone, that he does not have to visit Carl anymore. Before the visits he always had indigestion; afterward he sometimes wet his pants. Still, Arnold always believed what Sarah Miller never believed—that Carl was still finding himself, that one day he would return home, a normal young man.

She watches Mr. Barton wheel garbage pails to the curb and chain them to a tree. She remembers when Mr. Barton's daughter, Susan, was the only black child in the building. She would watch her play catch on the sidewalk with Carl. She would watch her skipping rope and eating candy bars. She wonders if it is better to have a son like Carl or a daughter like Susan, with her stiff yellow hair that birds could nest in, her sequined dresses, the men in black leather jackets and sunglasses who drive her around in long, gleaming cars.

The following evening, there is a knock at the door. Her sister, Rosalind, and her brother-in-law, Sidney, stand there.

"All right," Sidney says, when they have entered the apartment. "All right, why didn't you tell us?"

"Tell you what?"

"Come off it, Sarah," Rosalind says. "We know where he is this time."

"We thought something was wrong," Sidney says. "So we started phoning city hospitals until we located him."

"You did *what?*" Sarah Miller says.

"Did you want us to find out from somebody else?" Rosalind asks. "Is that what you wanted?"

"I'll make you some tea," Sarah Miller says, and covers her mouth with her hand, to keep herself from laughing out loud.

"Do you know what your trouble is, Sarah?" Sidney asks. "Your trouble is that you won't accept the situation. Carl is a sick boy and he'll never be well, but you keep hoping for cures."

Rosalind takes her sister's hands in her own. "You're so alone, darling," Rosalind says. "Don't we know that? Don't you think we want to be with you when these tragedies strike? Don't we know you have nobody else in the world?"

"Her trouble is she doesn't know how to listen to people who care about her most. But the way I look at it is this," Sidney says. "In this world there are strong people and there are weak people. Carl would have been well if he'd wanted to be well. But he didn't want to. That's the way I look at it."

"That's why you always protected him, darling," Rosalind says. "Don't you see? That's why you always treated him as if he was fragile."

"Fragile?" Sidney says. "Don't make me laugh. If she really believed he was fragile she wouldn't have insisted he go to Arnold's funeral and say Kaddish, would she? I was against that, wasn't I?"

"You were against that," Sarah Miller says, surprised to hear the words she now speaks. "Only listen. What makes sense? Why should I tell you each time he goes in and each time he goes out, and each time he goes up and each time he goes down? Why should you call the hospitals when you can call me?"

"You made a mockery out of Arnold's funeral by having Carl there, looking the way he did," Sidney says.

"Arnold was his father," Sarah Miller says. "If Carl wanted to be at his father's funeral, he was going to be at his father's funeral."

"Look, Sidney," Rosalind says. "Sarah always does what she wants anyway, so let's have some tea and talk about happier things, all right?"

Rosalind takes her sister by the elbow, leads her to the kitchen. They prepare a pot of tea, then sit in the living room drinking tea and eating pound cake. Rosalind and Sidney talk about their three children, all of whom are married, and their seven grandchildren. They show Sarah Miller photographs. They invite her, again, to come and live with them in Great Neck. They invite her to go with them to New Jersey and Long Island the following weekend, to visit two of their children. They urge her not to visit Carl for a while, because it will only upset her, but they say that if she is determined to visit him, they will give up their plans and drive her from Brooklyn to Queens, to the hospital. Maybe, they suggest, he is happier when he's left alone with other patients. Sidney says he will speak to a man he knows, a member of his Masonic lodge, who will see to it that Carl does not get put away in a back ward, or transferred upstate. He will see to it that Carl gets good dental work if he needs it.

When Rosalind and Sidney are ready to leave, Sidney asks Sarah Miller if she needs money. She says no. Sidney takes a fifty-dollar bill from his wallet and slaps it down on the foyer table. Sarah Miller finds herself wanting to laugh again. Rosalind says what she has often said before: that she and Sidney put a lot of pressure on Herbie when he was young, but he turned out fine, didn't he? She says that Sarah Miller never put pressure on Carl, and he broke, so what did it prove? Can a parent *not* love a child? Sidney is right. There are strong people and there are weak people.

Sarah Miller smiles.

"But I'll tell you something you don't know, since from the way you laugh at me, you seem to know so much already," Rosalind says. They are standing in the hallway, outside Sarah Miller's apartment. "I think you didn't tell us and made us find out ourselves because you like Carl the way he is."

"Roz, don't," Sidney says.

"No," Rosalind says. "It's about time she faced up to the truth. I think you like Carl the way he is, and you always did. That's what I think. The same way you liked Arnold the way he was."

"Roz, enough," Sidney says. "Please."

"All right then." Rosalind steps back. "I only thank God Sidney and I didn't need the money, so we said to let you have the building from Poppa after he died. 'Let her be well and use it for other things besides doctors' is what we said. But the truth, my dear sister, is that you like having weak men around so you can pick them up and make them well. Only when they get well, you like to make them sick again."

"I always gave Poppa a hot meal," Sarah Miller says.

"You *what*—?" Rosalind blinks.

Sarah Miller laughs. She looks past her sister and brother-in-law to the staircase. "Sometimes he called Momma a Cossack," she says. "Did you know that? 'I married a Cossack,' he would say to me. Poppa was a sweet man. Very sweet—and wonderfully ineffectual. But he was very gentle with Carl, even though Carl couldn't speak Yiddish with him. And also, for the record, I offered to give you half the money when I sold the building."

Sidney blows air through his lips. "You expected *us* to take from *you?*" He forces a laugh. "That'll be the day!"

"We'll call tomorrow," Rosalind says, and kisses her sister on the cheek. "We're sorry about Carl. Really."

Sidney kisses her. "Lock your door," he says.

From an apartment to their left, two teenage black boys emerge, wearing wide-brimmed felt hats. Instead of going directly down the stairs, one boy veers out of his way and brushes against Sidney. Sidney tells him to watch where he's going. From the boy's sleeve, there is a flash of silver and a switchblade knife clicks open, the blade pointed at Sidney's stomach. Rosalind screams. Sarah Miller sighs and tells the boy to stop fooling around or she'll tell his mother on him. The knife disappears. The two boys descend the stairs, laughing.

"You're crazy," Rosalind says. "You're as crazy as Carl, to live here."

"Are you all right?" Sarah Miller asks Sidney. His face is pale. "I'll get you a glass of water."

Rosalind takes Sidney's arm. "Come," she says. "There's no use talking to her. Didn't I tell you before?"

"Are you all right?" Sarah Miller asks again. "I'll get you some water. Would you like some water? Or a pill? I have pills left over from Arnold."

Sidney opens his mouth, but no words come. Rosalind tugs at his sleeve. "Enough," she says. "Come."

"Pills for high blood pressure," Sarah Miller says. "Your blood pressure might be up after something like this. You're not used to it anymore."

Sidney coughs and turns. He starts down the stairs. Rosalind follows.

"Lock the door!" Rosalind calls over her shoulder. "And about what I said—forget it. We're all very upset. Why shouldn't we be upset? We were his godparents, after all, weren't we?"

"You were his godparents," Sarah Miller says.

A half hour later, when she is already in bed, there is another knock at the door. Mr. Barton has come to ask if everything is all right. He heard screaming. Mr. Barton sits in the living room and she tells him what happened. He begins to talk about his daughter, about the black market for illegitimate children, about how much money he has in the bank. She notices that he is staring at the belt of her robe, and she pulls it tighter. She does not offer him tea. He tells her that an aunt of his lived in a state mental hospital, in Rockland, for thirty-six years and that he used to visit her regularly, every other Sunday afternoon, until she died. He tells her that he has not been to church since the first time his daughter let one of her babies be given away.

Sarah Miller notices that he is holding a hammer in his left hand. For an instant she imagines that he will try to force his affections upon her and that, in the course of their struggle, she will grab the hammer and hit him on the head with it. She imagines that he will plead with her to be kind to him, and that, afterwards, she will have to move from the building. She imagines him in his cellar apartment, drinking wine and reading the Bible.

He reminds her to bang on the pipes four times if she ever needs anything. Then he leaves. Sarah Miller locks the door behind him and goes into Carl's room. She pulls down the window shade. She sits at Carl's desk and writes out a list of the things she will bring to him on the weekend. She takes his old slide rule out of its leather case and plays with it for a few seconds, watching the numbers change positions under the rectangle of clear plastic. She gets sheets and a pillowcase, then strips Carl's bed and puts on fresh linens, in case the doctors decide to let him come home.

Later, when Carl telephones collect, Sarah Miller accepts the call. He tells her that he is feeling much better. She tells him she will be able to bring everything he asked for, except the Cuban cigars. Carl laughs and tells her he knows he was upset and not making sense when she visited, but that she will be surprised at how good he'll look when she comes next Saturday. At once, despite herself, her heart fills with hope. It happens, she tells herself. Sometimes, after many years, they suddenly get well.

"And listen, Carl," she says. "I'll see you on Saturday. There's only one thing," she adds.

"Yes?"

"Don't disappoint me, all right?" She waits, but he does not reply. "You know what I mean," she says, and hangs up.

She imagines Arnold standing by her side, shaking his head, asking her why she had to say what she said to Carl.

She hears noise, coming from the hallway, but she does not bother to see what is going on. Instead, she sits in the living room, sipping what is left of her tea, and seeing herself again, her back pressed against the wall, while her father falls down the stairs. She is holding her schoolbooks to her chest, and she is aware, for an instant, that she is feeling quite happy. She is looking past her father, at her mother's face—triumphant, enraged, smiling—and she sees that, if only for a moment, she is smiling too.

This Third Life

T*here was a life before children, and there was a life with children . . . and then, glory be, there was a life after children.* The words repeated themselves inside her head, and she thought too: I am forty-one years old, both my parents are in good health, all four of my grandparents are alive and well. I am a bright, attractive forty-one-year-old woman whose children have left home, I am beginning a new life—this third life—and if genes count for anything, I have not yet, wondrous fact, lived even *half* my life.

The plane had begun its descent into Reykjavik, and Ellen Kaplowitz, née Sherman, pressed her forehead to the window. She enjoyed the feel of cold, hard glass against skin and bone, and she enjoyed watching the dawn—the rising sun that floated above the landscape of Iceland. And she was enjoying, as much, the words she had conjured up to describe her three lives, for words did not come easily to her, and when she found words that could make sense of life—words she might be willing to utter aloud without the fear of embarrassment that usually seized her—she felt proud of herself as if of one of her own children.

For most of her life Ellen had been almost pathologically shy. Thus she had been relieved six hours before, at Logan International Airport, in Boston, to hear the elderly man who sat beside her speak to the Icelandair flight attendants in what she assumed was their native tongue. She had prepared words—questions and answers—for use should the man have wanted to exchange ordinary pleasantries: *I'm going to Germany to visit old friends for two weeks, and I'm hoping to take in some of the sights.*

What she saw no need to say to anyone, though, was that she was going to Freiburg, Germany, to visit Kerstin and Paul Kuhlman and their two children—to visit a woman who, fourteen summers before, had come to Northampton, Massachusetts as Ellen's *au pair* when Ellen's children were the ages, five and three, Kerstin's children were now. And she was also going to Germany to fulfill a vow she had made to herself while taking a course on the Holocaust at her synagogue a dozen years before—three months after her husband Danny had left her: that, if she and the children survived one another, in the first year following her children's leave-taking, she would journey across the ocean to visit one of the death camps.

Ellen closed her eyes and imagined the curve of the globe upon which the plane would, in a few moments, set down. Her visual memory rarely failed her, and so she did not need to continue to stare at low volcanic mountains, deep orange-gold rays of morning sun, or the mossy surface of this sparsely inhabited island. She knew she would be able to recall—and retrieve—the sight whenever she wished.

There was a term for her condition, a therapist had recently informed her, but then, these days, there were terms for everything: high-sounding phrases that made *disorders* or *syndromes* out of what she regarded as life's common anxieties and struggles. And whether her inability, in most situations, to be able to say what she thought or felt was an aphasia, or a neurosis, or something in between, what she had concluded was that she had come to like the fact that, when it came to words, she *was* profoundly inhibited. In an excessively noisy world, she reasoned, excessive timidity could not be *all* bad.

The plane was in its final approach, its belly nearly grazing the surface of the sea. The metallic highlights on the waves below were blindingly bright—more silver than gold now—and her mind, too, was bright, with pictures: of Kerstin fourteen years before, playing with Anne and David, Ellen's daughter and son, on backyard swings; of Anne and David—Anne now a junior at Tufts, David in his first year at MIT—at the airport, David's head on Anne's shoulder, tears streaming down his cheeks; of photos Kerstin had sent Ellen through the years—of Kerstin's wedding, of her honeymoon with Paul, of Kerstin's and Paul's two children.

Ellen turned toward the man next to her, prepared to make small talk (Did he have family here? Was he continuing on to Frankfurt?), only to discover that he was staring ahead wide-eyed, his neck slick with sweat, his sun-dried skin—was he a fisherman? a farmer?—drained of color.

The plane's wheels touched ground, its engines roaring into reverse. The man's mouth opened wide, in an oval of panic. He turned to Ellen and, without thinking, she put her hand on top of his. "It's all right," she said. "You're home."

What, she wondered, would she do with the rest of her life? She walked through this shamelessly beautiful city—with its clean, cobblestoned streets, its handsomely restored fourteenth- and fifteenth-century buildings, its canals, beer gardens, and outdoor cafes, Freiburg seemed unreal: a meticulously crafted movie set for a modern version of the ideal medieval German city—and she wondered how it could be, little more than a half century since the end of World War Two, that a Jew could be walking here freely. And how could it be, nine days into her fourteen-day sojourn, she asked herself, that she had not yet made arrangements to visit Dachau, the concentration camp nearest to Freiburg?

Ellen did not *want* to go to Dachau. Though the museum there was excellent, Paul had informed her, the buildings themselves—barracks, crematoria, gas chambers—like the medieval buildings in Freiburg's inner city, bombed at the end of the war, were reconstructions. The prospect of walking through a concentration camp with groups of high school students and other tourists as if through some Disneyland of the Holocaust, seemed almost silly to Ellen—an experience that could only trivialize an event it was intended to memorialize. Still, she did not see how she could *not* go.

Though, in the early years of their marriage, Danny had tried to explain away her intense feelings about Judaism in terms of her childhood, she had never bought his argument. We were always, she believed—and weren't their own children the living proof?—so much more than the mere vector of parental and genetic forces. Now, however, she wondered if he had not been more perceptive than she had been willing to admit.

When Ellen had become pregnant with Anne, she was in her sophomore year at the University of Massachusetts. Danny had been her professor for a course in modern American literature, and after quinine pills, hot baths, and horseback riding had not dislodged the fetus, they had decided to marry. She had been the number two player on the varsity tennis team, and her romance with Danny had begun on the tennis courts; he had come to her matches, suggested they play sometime ("Let's put the court back in courtship, yes?" he said, the first time, alone with her on the courts, they kissed). And so she had fallen in love, dropped out of school, converted to Judaism, married, and, four months after the wedding, given birth to Anne.

Despite the difficulties that came during and after her divorce (checks for child support had come irregularly, and then, as Danny drifted further west, from one temporary teaching job to another, not at all), she had come to feel grateful to him for what she believed were the two great gifts of her life: her children, and Judaism.

When, twenty-one years before, she told Danny she wanted to convert, he had laughed at her. Why would *anyone* want to do such a thing? he asked, assuming she was as estranged from her religion as he was from his. He had been correct about her estrangement, but not in the way he thought. Raised in a small Ohio town as a Southern Baptist, Ellen had always found the obsession with sin and fear, both at home and in church, quite literally god-awful. Then, at the age of thirteen, when she read *The Diary of Anne Frank*, she fell in love with Anne, and was overwhelmed by emotions she had never before known.

Though she spoke to no one about her feelings (doubtless the secrecy surrounding them made them more precious to her), she went often to her local library, searching out other books about Jews and Judaism. When, years later, in Danny's home on Friday nights, his mother lit candles and his father chanted blessings over wine and bread—and when she sat down to a Sabbath meal with his family (a family that, in Danny's words, had had cousins, aunts, and uncles chopped up for Hitler's barbeque), she found herself more than enchanted. This, she decided—a life wherein the days and years were marked by rituals that took place at home and not in church—was what she wanted for herself, for Danny, for their children.

After the wedding, she took pleasure in seeing Danny return, little by little, to his parents' ways—to the observing of the Sabbath, and of holidays. At the time, she thought her own example—the course of study she undertook with the rabbi for her conversion, the evening courses she took at their synagogue afterwards—had helped encourage him. Now, walking the streets of Freiburg, she remembered repeating to him what she had learned and thought he would find praiseworthy: that though Jews considered themselves a chosen people—a notion Danny despised—they were not chosen for anything like genetic or racial purity, since Jews had always accepted converts, whatever their nationality or race, as their own. In fact, it was considered a transgression to remind a convert that he or she had ever *not* been a Jew.

But what, besides her religion and her children, Ellen now wondered, did she believe in—what did she *know?*—that could become the basis for a life *without* children? The things she knew about—Judaism, tennis, raising children, housekeeping—seemed useless, and the jobs she had taken to support herself and the children after Danny's departure—part-time secretarial work, grunt work in supermarkets, motels, and shopping centers—were deadly dull. She could return to the university and complete her degree, of course. But then what? She would be nearly forty-five by the time she graduated, and who would want to hire a forty-five-year-old woman? The predictable jobs—teaching, library work, social work—were, in a region overflowing with faculty wives and graduate students, few and far between, and they held little appeal. She had spent her second life raising her own children—why spend the third helping raise other people's children?

The evening before, on what had become their nightly after-dinner walk through town (while Paul did the dishes and prepared the children for bed), Ellen and Kerstin had been reminiscing about Kerstin's summer in Massachusetts, and Ellen had found herself telling Kerstin about her three lives, and about what she thought she might yet do with the years ahead. The possibilities she kept coming to—how Jewish could one get, yes? she laughed—were those of doctor, lawyer, or rabbi. She explained to Kerstin the ways in which, given her shyness, she imagined she might make these professions her own: how, if a doctor, she could be a pediatrician (for she would feel confident talking with children, and with parents of children), or if a lawyer, one who practiced family law (preparing briefs, but not herself being a court lawyer), or if a rabbi, one who did research on historical and ethical issues (working either for other rabbis, or for a rabbinical school). Ellen had always been an excellent student; if she persevered and completed her studies by the age, say, of fifty, she might still have two or three productive decades left. But why, Kerstin asked then, become a doctor or lawyer when you can *marry* one?

They were walking along the Kanonenplatz—a large fortress-like plaza just outside the old city, in the first range of hills that led to the higher elevations of the Black Forest—and, surprised by Kerstin's question, Ellen felt her tongue double on itself, closing down the opening to her throat, and when she stumbled, drool had oozed from both her mouth and nose.

Kerstin held her then, wiped away the spit, led her to a bench. The evening sky was ice-blue, streaked with feathery tints of lavender and green, and Ellen looked beyond the towers and roofs of Freiburg's old city, and beyond the Black Forest, to where the Vosges mountains, in France, were visible. Kerstin smoothed Ellen's hair, asked Ellen why she was making herself think in such impractical ways.

"When I lived with you and Danny, I envied you your long blond hair," Kerstin said. "Mine is—how do you say?—*mouse* brown, yes? But I would go to sleep wishing I might wake up with your golden hair, your blue eyes, your fair skin without blemish. Even now, you look like a most desirable woman of perhaps thirty. How do you manage it?"

Ellen smiled, shrugged, looked away.

"The many years of raising Anne and David by yourself," Kerstin continued, "and with Danny leaving you, and his damage. How *did* you stay so young and beautiful, my friend? Tell me please what was your secret."

"Suffering," Ellen replied.

Then she had laughed, and said she was of course joking—that raising the children on her own had been easier, in truth, than raising them with Danny—especially given all his playing around with students—and the children, God bless, had been full of life, never passive. Their lives had given her life.

Kerstin and Ellen held hands on their walk home, as German women often did, while Kerstin, sounding to Ellen like the Jewish mother she had never had, told her again that a beautiful woman could easily find a new husband, and, if she played her hand skillfully, a wealthy one too. Men were eternally shallow in that way, after all, Kerstin noted. A woman with a pretty face always had a great advantage. The years ahead, then, she predicted, were going to be splendid: filled with adventure, romance, travel, friends, grandchildren . . .

When, at breakfast the next morning—four days before her departure—Ellen announced that she had purchased a round-trip train ticket for Munich, and would visit Dachau the next day, Paul offered to accompany her. He had no scheduled classes, he knew the city well, having attended the university in Munich, and there was some research he could do in the Dachau archives. Dachau was not, he said, a place one should visit alone.

Kerstin asked Ellen if Paul had talked with her yet about the book he was writing. Ellen said he had not, and Kerstin explained that Paul had been working for nearly five years on a history of anti-Semitism in Freiburg, one which focused on how the city and university had treated its Jews during the Third Reich.

Paul said little, but after Kerstin left for work, Ellen asked him about his book. Instead of answering her question, Paul told her that he had been waiting for an opportunity to be alone with her so that he might apologize to her for Kerstin's behavior.

"But I really *am* interested," Ellen said. "I've been wondering, for example, if there are now Jews in Freiburg who lived here before the war?"

"Oh no," Paul said. "There are none who returned, but I am not apologizing for Kerstin telling you about my book. I am apologizing for her suggestion to you about finding husbands. In my opinion, I think that—how do you put it in your American idiom?—you can do better."

Ellen felt heat rise to her cheeks.

"In my opinion, you are a most intelligent, capable woman," Paul continued, "and I do not think Kerstin meant to offend. Kerstin loves you as I do, and shares my warm and admiring regard for you."

Ellen wanted to tell him she would be pleased if he could regard her with a bit *less* admiration. She wanted to tell him she was proud to know him, and to feel that, like Kerstin, he was family to her. But she remained silent.

Paul smiled at her, and spoke: "Heidegger was rector here during the early years of the Nazi era," he said, "and on his own initiative he collaborated in the dismissal of Jewish faculty. Hannah Arendt, when a young woman of less than twenty years, was his mistress, as is by now common knowledge. Contrary to the situation in your nation, you see, the universities in Germany, even before Hitler, were—how do you say?—mighty hothouses: of racism and of Romanticism, and thereby easy prey for Nazi propaganda. Forty percent were party members, while the rest were compliant, yes? Did you notice, for example, the inscription in stone above the classroom building I teach my courses in? *Dem Ewigen Deutschtum*—which we might translate as 'To Eternal Germanness.' Inscribed there in 1934—and now and then without protest."

Ellen was puzzled. "Now *as* then—?" she asked.

"Thank you. Yes—now *as* then, there were no protests. I am working with a group of students to have the inscription removed, but our administration says this would only call attention to a matter better left to rest. It is the German way. As Chancellor Kohl has put it, our generation has the blessing of being born too late—*die Gnade der spaten Geburt*—by which he means those born after 1945 bear not the responsibility for what happened here eternally."

While Paul talked, presenting her with facts and theories concerning what he saw as the persistence of things endemic to something that *was* the essential German character, Ellen felt the muscles in her throat soften, and she found herself offering her own observations, and, after a while, and without self-consciousness, repeating for Paul what she had said to Kerstin about the choices that lay in wait for her.

That night, after she and Kerstin returned from their walk, and the children were asleep, Kerstin excused herself, leaving Ellen alone in the living room with Paul, so they could plan their trip.

Although more than two hundred thousand prisoners passed through Dachau, fewer than thirty-five thousand died there, Paul informed her. Dachau had not, in fact, been a true death camp, he explained. The gas chambers, for example, were never employed because, as some theorized, of the camp's proximity to Munich. Munich had, as he assumed she knew, been the birthplace of National

Socialism, and some historians speculated that Dachau had served primarily as a way station to the death camps in the East because Hitler did not want the ugliness of excessive blood and death to make its home close to his favorite German city.

Also, Paul wanted her to know, it had been Kerstin's suggestion that he accompany her to Dachau.

Ellen smiled, but said nothing.

"Kerstin has also made another suggestion," Paul continued. "Since the journey itself takes four hours, plus the train and bus to Dachau, she has proposed that you and I stay in Munich overnight. I would, thus, have time also to show to you what I love in Munich: the *Englischer Garten*, the fine museums. I have taken the liberty of making a hotel reservation."

"That's thoughtful of you," Ellen said. She paused, then decided to speak to him of her ambivalence. "The truth is, though, that I've been delaying the trip till the last minute because I'm not really sure anymore that I *want* to go," she said. "I feel that I *should* go, yet now that I'm here, I—well, I just don't know."

She felt, suddenly, flustered. "What I do know, though," she went on quickly, "is that I surely will not be good company for you—that I won't have much to say once we're there."

"Of course," Paul said. "What words exist for such horror? As your Mister Elie Wiesel has said, 'How can there be any life after the camps?' But please, then, tell me, Ellen, why you insist still on going there?"

"Because I'm a Jew," Ellen said.

"But not really," Paul said.

Ellen blinked. "Excuse me? I *am* a Jew, Paul. I was not Jewish before my marriage, but I am a Jew now."

"Oh yes," Paul said. "Of course. What I mean is—well, *look* at you. Just look at your hair, your eyes—"

Ellen closed the eyes of which he spoke, but saw only darkness; when she opened them, Paul was still sitting across from her, talking.

It had been Kerstin's suggestion that he accompany her to Dachau not only for the reasons already stated, he was saying, but because he found Ellen a most attractive woman. He and Kerstin had an agreement—perhaps *arrangement* was a better word—concerning the freedom they granted to each other in marriage. He would not insult a woman of Ellen's quality with a vulgar approach, but he sensed that his feelings toward her were reciprocated. He had seen it in her eyes, and in the way heat moved from her body to his when in proximity. Therefore, he had reserved only one room at the hotel. He did not expect Ellen to give her assent at once, but he hoped she would consider his proposal seriously. If she rejected his offer, it would in no way affect their ability to be friends, or the great affection and regard he and Kerstin held for her.

His words came to her across the living room as if, quite literally, she thought, they were arriving from a distant land. She stood, bowed her head slightly. "I appreciate the regard you have for me," she said, "and I will consider your offer."

In Strasbourg, her two suitcases checked at the train station, she bought a guidebook to the city, and spent the morning seeing the sights: the church and its famous clock, the old city, the bridges, the towers, the canals. Although she had slept for less than two hours (shortly after four a.m. she had walked to the train station, then waited there until dawn for the slow morning train west), she felt little fatigue.

A few minutes before noon, she left the old city, walking toward the university and away from the more heavily touristed areas. She entered a small restaurant, but its dining room, decorated in soft oranges and golds, was deserted. She felt as if she had, without being invited, entered someone's home, and she was about to leave when an elderly French woman—the *propriétaire*, as she would learn, who owned the restaurant with her husband—appeared from behind a curtain. Ellen asked if the restaurant was open. Of course, the *propriétaire* said, and she led Ellen to a table.

Nearly two hours later, Ellen was still sitting at her table, sipping coffee. She could not recall ever before having eaten by herself in anything other than a fast-food restaurant, and she was surprised at how easy it had been to do so—as if it were the most natural, ordinary thing in the world. She had chosen the four-course menu of the day—the *quiche Lorraine*, the *coq au vin*, the cheese (Munster and Camembert), and the *crème caramel*—along with a half-bottle of red wine. It was, she decided, the most elegant meal she had ever had.

She had read through the guidebook, watched the other patrons, asked the *propriétaire* about hotels and *chambres d'hôtes* (she would stay two nights, then take a train to Frankfurt for her return flight home), inquired about the city's synagogue.

The moment that would stay with her above all, however, had occurred between the first and second courses. The *propriétaire* had taken away Ellen's plate, along with her knife and fork, and had returned several minutes later carrying a plate upon which lay, not food, but a freshly folded pale gold napkin—and upon the napkin, a bright new silver place setting which she placed in front of Ellen—and Ellen decided that she was going to consider this moment the true beginning of her third life.

Though she hardly thought of Paul and Kerstin while she ate—in truth, she had not thought much about *anything* during the previous two hours except for the meal she was eating and the city she intended to explore—she did acknowledge the truth of some of what Paul had said to her.

She *had* found him attractive, and had the opportunity not presented itself whereby he had come to say to her the very stupid things he had in fact said, she knew she would have found his offer attractive too. She was, after all, a bright, attractive forty-one-year-old woman whose children had left home, and whose new life was beginning. And who could tell, after all, who she might be and what she might yet discover in this life.

His Violin

Three weeks and one day after the week of *shiva* is over—at the end of *sheloshim*, the prescribed thirty days of restricted mourning that follow on the week of mourning, during which time I have neither shaved, had my hair cut, nor attended any festive gathering—I take a taxi downtown, to where my nephew Michael has his office.

Michael and I both live in West Palm Beach, Florida now. I live in Century Village, a senior-citizen city, with fifteen thousand other retired people, most of whom are elderly Jews. Michael, his wife Ruth, and their three children live in an apartment house on Flagler Drive, overlooking the Intracoastal Waterway. Michael is a lawyer, and he saw to all the details concerning my brother Simeon's burial.

I tell Michael that I have come to give him a secret. He laughs. Lately I've been telling people that my new hobby is collecting family secrets, and that before I die, I hope to collect *all* the family secrets. During the week we sat *shiva* in my apartment, I asked each of my sisters—along with their husbands, their children, the cousins who came to visit—if they had a secret they wanted to give me: something they'd never told anybody else, something, perhaps, of which they were especially ashamed.

Michael sits next to me, and I ask if he remembers the time he came to me, when we lived in Brooklyn, with a Classic Comic of *The Corsican Brothers*.

"It was my favorite," he says. "But remember how my mother always used to make me do something else if she caught me reading comic books?"

I don't answer his question. "So I've changed my mind," I say. "What I've decided is that instead of collecting secrets, I want to give some away, all right? Your bringing the comic book—that was part of what made me think of what I wanted you to have."

He picks up the phone, tells his secretary to hold his calls. Some of his plaques and trophies, from when he was a star athlete in high school and college, now decorate his office. There are also, on his desk, pictures of his wife, and of their children. I was Michael's favorite uncle, he was my favorite nephew. Unlike his mother, my sister Pearl, Michael did not chastise me for not going north for the funeral. Simeon had spent most of his adult life in a mental hospital in Queens. If I hadn't seen him alive for over two years—since I moved down here—why, I reasoned, should I have journeyed north to see him dead?

"I used to think Simeon and I were like the Corsican brothers," I say. "That we were somehow joined invisibly the way Siamese twins are, but that where we were joined, instead of in the foot, was in the heart."

Michael smiles. "I guess I loved the story so much when I'd read about one of them being in pain or in danger and the other brother feeling it—even though he was hundreds of miles away—was because, being an only child, I sometimes wished I could have a brother."

"Why I am here," I say. "Why I am here is because I want to tell you about the happiest moment of my life. I used to think that the happiest moment of my life was when I first saw Simeon in the bedroom at Momma's breast, after he was born, but I decided that Simeon was right about envy—about even the ordinary kind of jealousy I must have felt in that moment. The happiest moment of my life, I decided instead was the time Poppa and I went with Simeon to see Mr. Langenauer.

"Momma had bought a piano for Pearl—she sold it years ago, before you were born—and what I loved most was when Simeon would tiptoe into the living room and, like Pearl's teacher, whenever Pearl hit a wrong note, Simeon would leap up onto the piano bench and slap her hands. Well. You know all about Simeon's talent. Pearl always talked lovingly of the talent he had when he was a child, about how he could go to the piano and play any melody he heard—from *shul*, from what he heard Pearl play, from what Poppa sang with the men on Shabbos during *shaleshudes*—and he could play with both hands.

"'Maybe he's another Paderewski,' Momma declared, and in this, you see, Poppa defied her. He wanted Simeon's gifts to come from him, I think. So instead of giving Simeon lessons at the piano, one day he brought home a small violin. I'd never seen Simeon's eyes sparkle the way they did when Poppa opened the brown wrapping paper, then the newspaper, and then the black leather case and handed the instrument to Simeon. Simeon took the instrument, and plucked it—he looked into its opening, and held it to his chest as if it were a doll. That first night he wrapped it in a blanket and slept with it.

"Momma was furious—we already had a piano and a piano teacher, one who would teach Simeon too when his legs were longer, she said. She railed against Poppa for spending the money on the violin, and on the teacher, who was a poor musician himself, a young violinist who gave lessons to boys and girls without Simeon's gift, and who must have charged pennies.

"Then one day the music teacher waited until it was dark—until Poppa came home, to have a talk with him, and the next day the three of us—Simeon, Poppa, and I—were going across Brooklyn Bridge together on the streetcar, and all the way uptown, near where the Metropolitan Museum of Art is. Simeon was five years old and I was nine. We both wore our best knickers. Mr. Langenauer was the director of a musical conservatory whose name I do not remember. He lived in a beautiful town house just off Fifth Avenue, and a servant came to the door to let us in. Poppa whispered to me that Mr. Langenauer was Jewish, and it surprised me. I had not known Jews could live in such houses.

"We sat in a room that had an enormous piano and Mr. Langenauer played notes and asked Simeon to name the notes. Then he asked Simeon to take out his violin, after which he would play a melody on the piano and he would ask Simeon to repeat it on the violin. Then he asked Simeon to play the same melody in a different key. All the while that Poppa and I sat, our hats on our heads, on silk-covered chairs, Mr. Langenauer showed no reaction. He had a pointed white beard and piercing gray eyes. When he spoke I hardly understood what he said. But Simeon did. He was thrilled, he was unafraid, he was lost in the musical games, and he was eager to please.

"Mr. Langenauer set up a music stand for Simeon and put music on it, and then the two of them played together—a movement from an early Mozart sonata Simeon had not heard before, in which, at first, the violin is really playing the accompaniment for the piano—and only when that was done did Mr. Langenauer react. Then the ice in his gray eyes melted, the pursed lips became soft and full, and the severe Germanic teacher vanished. Mr. Langenauer lifted Simeon up by both arms and kissed him on both cheeks.

"'*Wunderkind!*' he exclaimed. Then he sat Simeon down gently, and left the room—still without talking to Poppa—and came back a short while later with a large bar of chocolate, which he presented to Simeon.

"'This boy may become a fine musician,' he said to Poppa. 'He certainly has the talent for it. Let him hear some good singing whenever you can, but do not force music upon him. When the time comes for serious study, bring him to me, and I shall be glad to supervise his artistic education.'

"That, I have decided, was the happiest moment in my life," I tell Michael. "Simeon put his violin away, opened the wrapper of his chocolate bar, and gave me half. He was a very generous boy, even then. When we left, he carried the chocolate bar, and I carried his violin.

"Mr. Langenauer said to Poppa to bring Simeon back to him in two years' time. But tell me what you think, Michael—I came here for your good counsel, yes?—was God jealous of our happiness? Fifteen months after this, Mr. Langenauer died. Poppa showed the article in the newspaper to us. In the article it said that Mr. Langenauer had been the foremost pupil in America of the great Joseph Joachim, a violinist who had been director of a conservatory in Berlin. Joachim had trained Rubenstein, when Rubenstein was a little boy.

"Momma said that she didn't wish this Langenauer dead, but that she had never understood how Poppa expected to *shlep* Simeon to Manhattan every week for lessons—he had trouble enough *shlepping* himself to and from work each day. So what I think is that if it had been a few years earlier—before Simeon was born, and before Momma became so bitter—Poppa might have been strong enough to . . ."

I stop talking, hoping Michael will say something, but he remains quiet. "As we used to say," I say to him, "If my aunt had had balls, we would have called her my uncle, yes? So what's the use, really, is the conclusion I've come to. Because everything changed after that. Simeon kept playing, and Momma even got him a teacher—Momma, not Poppa—but it was never the same."

"I'm sorry," Michael says.

"I must have been very angry with Poppa," I say. "But who could have known it then? He was who he was the way I was who I was and Simeon was who he was. And even if Mr. Langenauer had lived, who knows if Simeon's life would have been different?"

"Or yours."

"Or mine," I agree. I stand. "Listen. You must have things to do."

"I'm glad you gave me the story."

"Don't mention it. What could I do with it anyway, after all these years? And it may not look it, but remembering Poppa and Simeon back then made me happy again for a few moments—not the way I once was, of course—but it made me happy to share the story with you."

"You wouldn't mind—later on—if I told the story to Ruth, or to the children?"

"Of course not," I say. "It's your secret now. You do what you want with it."

I go to the door and try to leave, but the door is stuck. Michael comes and opens it. I realize that I am hoping he will say something else—tell me, perhaps, what he thinks I am feeling, or what he is feeling toward me—but he says nothing. Then, as I go through the doorway, he catches my arm, bends down, and kisses me on the cheek. His eyes are moist, and when his lips move away I remember the way I felt when I was a little boy and I would wait at our front door for Poppa to come home from work so that he would be able to bend down and kiss me before he got to Simeon.

Lev Kogan's Journey

On the evening that he had long awaited, a Friday evening when the synagogue of which he was president—Congregation B'nai Israel, in Northampton, Massachusetts—would officially welcome into its midst Lev and Gita Kogan, two Russian Jewish emigrés from the city of St. Petersburg, Max Davidoff arrived home from work to find Lev standing in the center of the living room, a black velvet cape draped around his shoulders. The cape belonged to Davidoff's daughter, Sharon, who was a senior at Smith College, and Lev was swirling the cape about in wide circles. Sharon, seated at the piano, was laughing. Davidoff's wife, Harriet, sat on the couch, her hands in her lap.

In his heart Davidoff wished he could love Lev as much now as he had during those months in which he had worked to bring him to America. Seventeen months before, when he received a letter from Sharon, who was spending her junior year abroad in Israel, telling him about the Kogans and suggesting that Davidoff have Congregation B'nai Israel sponsor their emigration to America, Davidoff had been elated.

Sharon struck several chords, Lev shouted something in Russian, stamped his boots on the carpeting, and twirled about.

"Please," Davidoff said. "I'm home."

Lev stopped abruptly, so that the bottom edge of the cape, weighted down with pieces of lead, nearly swept a pair of porcelain doves from the coffee table. Harriet gasped. Lev bowed down to Davidoff, took Davidoff's hand, and drew it toward his lips. Davidoff tried to pull back. Lev kissed the air above Davidoff's knuckles. "Good Shabbos to you, dear friend," he said.

"Please," Davidoff said again. He turned to his wife. "Have you lit the candles? Is it already Shabbos?"

"No," she said. "We waited for you."

Davidoff nodded. "Yes," he said to Lev. "This is a night we have looked forward to for many months."

Lev drew the cape across his face with his right arm, so that only his eyes showed. Inside the white velvet lining of the hood, his skin, a brownish-yellow color, looked as if it had been stained with nicotine. "Le Dracule!" Lev stated. "Le Dracule! A Jew! A Zhid!"

Sharon kissed Davidoff on the cheek. Her long, wheat-colored hair was rolled into a bun on top of her head.

"Smile, Daddy," she whispered. "He's only trying to please you, can't you see?"

"Good evening, Mister Davidoff." Davidoff turned and shook Gita's hand. She was a short, plump woman, dressed in a plain brown wool suit. She smiled broadly, revealing pink gums and a gold-capped front tooth.

"Forgive me," Davidoff said. "How have you been?"

Lev folded Sharon's cape and set it down on the piano bench. He put his arm around Davidoff's shoulder. "Is Lev only making joke?" He shook his head sideways. "Not at all, my friend. Have I told this to you, that still in villages they believe that Le Dracule is old Jew which sucks blood from Christian children for baking of Passover *matzot*?" Davidoff started to leave, but Lev held his arm. "How do I know this? I know this from when as a student I dug potatoes in villages and they found out that I am Jew and asked such things. Do you understand now why I bless you?"

Davidoff looked into Lev's face. "It was like that?" he asked. "It was really like that?"

"Why would I pull you the leg?" Lev asked. He dropped to his knees in front of Davidoff. "If not for you, dear friend —"

"Get up!" Davidoff snapped. "Get up! Please! Get up at once!"

He went upstairs, where he sat on the edge of his bed, irritated with himself for having lost control. For many months he had looked forward to this evening: to bring another Jew out of Russia and to do for him what Davidoff's own father and older brothers had done for him once upon a time—this had, in the beginning, been a dream come true.

He sat by the window and looked across the street, at Child Park—at the vast expanse of snow-covered lawns, the tall evergreens, the splendid bare trunks and branches of maples, birches, oaks. For a Jew to live freely in a beautiful New England town—oh how far we have come in America, he thought.

He thought also of the speech he would make within a few hours. Lev and Gita Kogan, he would say, were living examples of what the life of the Jew—the Wandering Jew of fact and of legend—had been like the world over for most of recorded history. American Jews, privileged and sheltered, knew little of this. It was their rare and good fortune to have been brought to these shores, or to have been born here, and to be living in what was surely one of the Golden Ages of Judaism.

Davidoff looked at his notes. Lev Kogan had been born in Vilna, in 1940. His father, a wealthy man before the war, had been saved from the Nazi concentration camps by the Communists. When the Russians occupied Vilna, in the spring of 1941, they had arrested him for his capitalist crimes and had sent him to Siberia. Lev was put into an orphanage. After the war the father and son were reunited. But Lev's mother, along with his three older sisters and two older brothers, had been killed by the *Einsatzgruppen* in one of the death pits at Ponary, ten kilometers outside Vilna. In 1953, two days before Lev's thirteenth birthday, Lev's father committed suicide by hanging himself. Lev returned to the orphanage, from which, at the age of fifteen, he was released and sent to a trade school in St. Petersburg to become an electrician.

Lev had spent eleven years in Soviet prisons and camps for anti-Soviet activities—for running an underground newspaper, for passing out Zionist literature. He had been interned in Morozov's Serbsky Institute of Forensic Psychiatry for three years. And he had, after the Yom Kippur War—the story that touched Davidoff most deeply—led a public demonstration on behalf of the state of Israel. He had appeared in court during the trial that followed, dressed in a *yarmulke*, *talis*, and *tephillin*. To all accusations made against him, he had, Sharon wrote, recited the same sentence, over and over again: *Shma Yisroel Adonai Elohenu Adonai Echod*—Hear O Israel the Lord our God the Lord is One.

Davidoff listened to the sound of Lev's laughter. He sighed. No matter what arguments he gave himself, he knew that the truth was that he neither liked nor trusted the man. But why not? He moved away from the window and found that he was thinking of his father and his four older brothers, all dead, and that he was, silently—a surprise—asking them for forgiveness. They had struggled, suffered, and worked—for ten, twelve, and fourteen hours a day—so that he might come to America, so that he might have the life none of them ever had.

Davidoff closed his eyes, and imagined his father's eyes staring back at him. He saw that his father was on his knees, and Davidoff wanted to call out to him, across the years, to get up, to rise, to stop crying.

His father embraced him, talking to him in Yiddish, and Davidoff remembered that he had not been able to find it in himself to return the embrace. He was eight years old. He remembered that he had stood there stiffly, as he was standing now, fifty-seven years later; he was frightened, he recalled, that this man who was a stranger to him—a man who had left Galicia to join his four other sons seven years before, when Davidoff himself was not yet a year old—would know of his anger, and would strike him.

In those first moments, when nothing happened—when the man let go of him and stood, and when others, who he soon learned were his brothers, came forward and kissed him and spoke to him in the English language—he found that his anger faded. Still, he had not embraced them.

He entered the dining room and saw the table set for the Sabbath meal—a white damask tablecloth, silver candlesticks, a silver wine goblet, two small challahs covered with a white napkin. He smiled, and when Lev returned his smile, he felt suddenly drawn toward the man as if to an old friend. He touched his daughter's forehead with his fingertips; she lowered her eyes while he gave her the traditional blessing, that the Lord look down upon her and bless her as He had blessed Sarah, Rebecca, Leah, and Rachel. He looked toward his wife, to indicate that she could light the candles, but she smiled and looked at Lev. Lev reached down and lifted a package from his chair.

"Gita and I would like, in smallest way, to thank you on night that symbolizes liberation." Lev handed the package to Davidoff.

Davidoff untied the ribbon, opened the package, and saw three leather-covered books. He lifted one of them and opened it: *History of the Jews in Russia and Poland: From the Earliest Times until the Present Day, Volume II*, by Simon M. Dubnow.

"It is first books I read after died my father," Lev said, "that make me understand what it means to be Jew, when such books were forbidden me."

Davidoff placed the books on the sideboard. "Thank you, Lev," he said. "Thank you."

He looked at Harriet and nodded, so that Harriet, understanding him, struck a match, lit the two Sabbath candles, covered her eyes, recited the blessing, then uncovered her eyes and—as if regarding a miracle—found the candles waiting there, already lit.

"You will read books I have found for you, and I hope you give me books also," Lev said, "so that we may learn from each other."

Davidoff raised the silver wine goblet. It was as if, he thought while he chanted the blessing over the wine, what he had remembered about his own arrival in America had wrought a small miracle; as if, while he was upstairs a few minutes before, his thoughts—his memory, his imagination—had brought about a change in Lev; as if another Lev—the true Lev—had finally arrived in America to take the place of the false. Davidoff drank the sweet wine and passed the goblet to his wife.

The next few weeks were, for Davidoff, among the happiest of his life. Every evening after supper Lev would come to Davidoff's house and, the kitchen table cleared, the two men would sit and study together. Davidoff taught Lev to read and write in Hebrew; he showed Lev how to put on *talis* and *tephillin* in the proper manner; he taught him the order of the prayers; he talked to him of Jewish history, culture, and customs—of all those things that had, until this moment in Lev's life, been denied to him. In the afternoons, while Davidoff worked at the men's clothing store he owned in downtown Northampton, it pleased him to know that his daughter was tutoring Lev in English, that his wife was shopping or cooking with Gita, and that Lev was happy with a job Davidoff had found for him—a position as an electrician's helper in a local construction company.

The Sabbath had always been for Davidoff a day of rest; now, by Lev's presence, its pleasures were multiplied. On Saturday morning, Lev would arrive early and the two men would eat breakfast together.

Then they would walk to synagogue. Gita, Harriet, and Sharon would arrive at services somewhat later, and when services were over, the five of them would return to Davidoff's house, eat lunch, and spend the afternoon together—taking walks, discussing the week's Torah portion, listening to Lev's descriptions of what was most fascinating of all to Davidoff: what his life as a Jew in the Soviet Union had been like.

Lev spoke of things he had learned from his father. He spoke of his great-great-grandfather, a scribe, who had touched Herzl's hand when Herzl had come to Kishinev during the first years of the century, after the pogroms there. He spoke of how some of his ancestors had been forced into twenty-five years' service in the tsar's army, and of how others had been forcibly baptized. He talked also of his life in the Serbsky Institute, in orphanages, prisons, labor camps.

Davidoff could not, it seemed, ever learn enough of what life had been like for Jews left behind in the country in which, sixty-five years earlier, he had been born. Lev had been tortured. He had, in coldest winter, worked without gloves or winter clothes, digging trenches for gas lines. And yet, he claimed, he himself had always believed that as a Soviet Jew he was a greatly privileged human being. For only Soviet Jews could legitimately hope to get out of Russia one day. The others—Ukrainians, Armenians, and those from the Baltic countries—did not have the state of Israel. They did not have the efforts of American Jews, and of men like Max Davidoff.

At the end of each Sabbath, after they had performed the *havdallah* ceremony and sniffed the fragrance of cloves from the spice box, Lev would never fail to tell Davidoff that to do as Jews had done for all time and in all places—to set aside one day each week as a day of rest, prayer, and study, and to thereby join himself with Jews everywhere—was the great privilege of his life, the true dream fulfilled.

One Saturday evening near the end of winter, when Davidoff was alone in the living room with Sharon, and when he started to speak with her about Lev, to share with her his feelings of pride and satisfaction, she grew quickly irritated.

"Oh, Daddy," she said, waving a hand at him. "Lev is just very extravagant, can't you see?"

"Extravagant?" Davidoff said. "I don't understand."

Sharon shrugged. "Extravagant," she repeated. "That's all." She set down her book, and left the room.

Perhaps she's jealous, Davidoff thought. She was, after all, an only child, and he was lavishing the kind of attention upon another that he had always lavished upon her. The truth, he knew, was that he had always indulged Sharon, who had come to him late in life, in the same way that his own father, from the time of his arrival in America, had indulged him. Nor did he believe that she had suffered for it. She had already been accepted into Harvard Law School. In less than a year she would leave Northampton. Perhaps soon after, Davidoff mused, she would meet a nice young man and marry. There would be a new home, visits, grandchildren ...

One Saturday morning in early spring, two weeks before the festival of Passover, Lev did not appear at Davidoff's home. Davidoff walked to the synagogue alone. When Sharon and Harriet arrived an hour later, Gita and Lev were not with them. Lev arrived during lunch, wearing his high army boots, his gray Russian army greatcoat, and a raspberry-colored Uzbek skullcap. Around his neck were old fox furs, the heads still attached. Lev spread his arms wide. "Mister Max Davidoff, how happy I am to greet you on special day!"

His cheeks flushed, Lev strode forward, embraced Davidoff, and kissed him on the mouth.

"Please," Davidoff said. "Have you eaten yet? Are you all right, Lev?"

"Do you not see?" Lev asked, and he turned in a circle. "Ah, my dear friend, we have much to talk about! So much."

"I was worried," Davidoff said softly.

Lev lifted Davidoff's *yarmulke* and pressed his lips to Davidoff's forehead. "There was never need to worry about Lev Kogan," he said. "He will survive all dangers. For references, you ask daughter, who has known me in two nations."

Davidoff stared at Sharon. "I'll vouch," Sharon said and, her mouth full, she began to laugh.

"Is it time to rest?" Lev asked, and answered: "It is time to rest." He placed several books on the sideboard. He smoothed the fox furs with his hand, then left the room.

After lunch Davidoff found Lev asleep on the couch, his boots off.

Lev opened one eye and smiled. He stood, sat beside Davidoff, and took his hand. "Tell, please, Mister Max Davidoff, about Frankists of whom I have been reading in books you gave. You are man of great learning. You will know what to tell me that I will not go astray."

Davidoff began to recite what he knew about the Frankists: that they were an eighteenth-century Polish sect that worshipped Jacob Frank as if he were the Messiah; that they were descended from those Jews who had previously worshipped the false messiah, Sabbatai Zevi. The Frankists had engaged in orgies and countenanced sexual excesses; they had been baptized; they had converted to Catholicism; they had even, in Lvov, defended, in collusion with the bishop, charges of blood libel against other Jews.

At this news, Lev stood. "Aha!" he exclaimed. "It is Le Dracule, do you not see? It is what I have thought! How many times have not Jews taken ways of host nation in outward style, to better preserve true Judaism in inner life? Was I not concealed while mother burned and father broke rocks? When we learned together of Marranos in Spain, after the expulsion of Jews, did we not admire their courage?"

"But the Marranos were different," Davidoff said. "The Frankists were not *forced* to abandon Judaism."

"There I agree with you," Lev said.

Davidoff closed his eyes. "Please," he said. "I'm tired. May we continue our talk another day? I'm not feeling well."

On Tuesday, at his store, Davidoff received a call from Lev's employer, informing him that Lev had not been at work for four days. At a board of directors meeting in the synagogue the following evening, when the subject of Lev and Gita came up, there was laughter and mumbling. Davidoff asked what the laughing was about. A man spoke from the back row and said that it seemed that Lev was indeed getting a very special education, and without having to pay tuition. He was seen in Fitzwilly's, a restaurant and bar frequented by Smith College students, regularly in the afternoons, surrounded by young women. He could be found, late in the evenings, in the lounges of their dormitories.

Davidoff warned the board about spreading evil rumors. He reminded them of the years Lev spent in Soviet camps and hospitals. Maybe, a board member suggested, to more laughter, to have let Lev loose on the Smith campus after being shut away was like setting a smorgasbord in front of a starving man.

The following evening, when Lev came by after supper, he asked if he and Gita were still welcome for the Passover *seders*. Davidoff said that they were. Lev put an arm around Davidoff. "You can believe what people tell you, or not," he said. "It is the same to me. But I know you will always be loyal friend and protector. You are more than father to me."

"What is it you want of me, Lev?" Davidoff asked.

"To talk with me," Lev replied. "To tell me if I am on right path or wrong path. Only to talk with me. But of late you pull away, and I want to draw you back." Davidoff nodded. "Listen to me, Max Davidoff. Does not prophet Elijah himself come to us on Shabbos disguised as stranger? Did not God disguise Himself in bushes, rocks, and fire, to test us?" Lev sat next to Davidoff. "Jacob Frank declared necessity for followers of adopting Christianity outwardly in order to keep true faith secret. Are not all religions, he asked, only stages through which believers pass, like men putting on different suits of clothes?"

"No," Davidoff said. "All religions are not like that. Judaism is not like that."

"Not for you," Lev said. "But think of history of Jew in Russia. Think of how we always, like God, conceal ourselves. I must find the child I was, when I, too, was disguised."

"But the Frankists were evil—" Davidoff began.

"*Evil!*" Lev declared. "That is just what I wished to hear from you. And yet, is that not what Jacob Frank himself believed—that the more one strews rotten fruit upon field, the richer will become land?" Lev held Davidoff's arm. "How beautiful the image! Was not father saved by those he despised? Are you not to me like father?"

"No," Davidoff said. "To be weak is not to be evil."

Lev covered his eyes with his right hand. "Sometimes I too am weak, Max Davidoff, yet when I tell you what is in heart, I feel you withdraw from me." He took Davidoff's hand in his own. "Why if God despised evil did He not choose to make us perfect from beginning? Was He also weak? Do you *like* me?"

Davidoff stood. "I don't feel well," he said.

Lev grasped Davidoff by the shoulders. "But you brought me here, Max Davidoff, don't you see? You brought me here to America."

Ten days later, on the evening that preceded the first day of Passover, Davidoff arrived home from synagogue to find his wife and daughter standing in the kitchen in one another's arms, weeping. Sharon dried her eyes and told Davidoff that she had hoped he would not have to know, but that she had decided, against her mother's judgment, that it was best to tell him the truth. She began weeping again, but softly, and though she swallowed some words, and choked on others, and interjected her news with apologies, Davidoff understood the basics: that she was pregnant, that Lev was the father, and that Sharon had already arranged, when the holidays were over, to have an abortion.

"It is time to begin the *seder*," he said when Sharon had collapsed in her mother's arms, and he turned away from his wife and daughter, went upstairs, and changed from his suit into his *kittel*, the long white robe his father had given to him when he married. Then he returned to the dining room and sat at the head of a table upon which were set out all the traditional foods—the bitter herbs, the parsley, the salt water, the hard-boiled eggs, the wine, the roasted lamb bone, the *charoses*, the *matzot*.

When Sharon put a hand on his arm, he pushed her away. "Sit in your place, Sharon. It is time to celebrate the going forth from Egypt."

"Oh, Daddy!" she said. "Just tell me what you *think*, for God's sake!" She shivered. "You're so *cold*, damn you. Tell me what to do. Tell me what you *want* from me! *Please*—"

"I want nothing."

"I'm sorry," she said. "All right? I'm sorry it happened. I'm sorry a thousand times. I'm sorry I wasn't more careful, only . . ."

"Only what?"

Sharon shrugged. "Only it's happened to lots of nice girls before. Lots of nice *Jewish* girls, too."

"We should begin the *seder*," Davidoff said. "We should celebrate the going forth from Egypt."

Sharon bent down toward her father. "And it won't be the first time for me either, do you hear that?" she said. "It won't be the first time! It won't be the first time!"

"That's all?" Davidoff asked. "You're through?"

Sharon rested her face against her mother's bosom. Davidoff looked at the candles, at Elijah's silver goblet, at the *seder* plate.

"Shh," Harriet said to Sharon. "It will be all right. You'll see. It will be all right."

"No," Davidoff said. "It will not be all right."

The doorbell rang. Davidoff turned. Lev and Gita stood in the doorway. Lev looked at Davidoff, then at Sharon, then back to Davidoff. "Ah, my friend," he began. "How I wish—"

Davidoff glared. "Please leave," he said. "There are trains from Springfield that can take you to New York City. You should go at once. Go to the Hebrew Immigrant Aid Society. They will place you elsewhere. They will care for you."

"I see that you are upset," Lev said, then shrugged, palms upward. "But sometimes, despite better selves, things happen. How I wish we could erase past, yet when I tried to speak with you, from heart—"

"Please take your wife and leave my home," Davidoff said. "I don't ever want to have to look at you again."

"But I was only doing what I thought you wished of me to do," Lev said. "Did you not inquire of me and ask what—" he glanced toward Gita "—what was impossible? Was I not like son to you? Were we not like family?"

"No," Davidoff said. "We were not."

"We must not rush into actions that will harm us more," Lev said. "We must to care for children of Israel. Believe me, I have argued with ceaselessness against daughter. And what, I ask of you, if Jacob Frank was right, that the world is unsown field?"

Sharon sighed. "Forget it," she said. "It was the same story in Israel—why I helped him. Lev Kogan, the Russian Jew—a most charming man. You can take my word for it."

"I do take your word," Davidoff said. "For I was charmed also."

"And now will you say I have been ungrateful, yes?" Lev moved closer to Davidoff. "But did I *ask* you to save me? Did father ask Communists to save him? Am I not allowed to be flesh like other men?"

Davidoff realized that he was listening carefully to Lev's words, and that he was believing none of them. He had been right, in the beginning, not to trust him.

"Please sit," Davidoff said to his wife and daughter, and he turned his back to Lev. "It is time to begin."

"Did I ask you to take me in?" Lev said. "You did what you for *your* desires, Mister Max Davidoff."

"True enough," Davidoff said, but he did not turn around.

Lev laughed, and when he did, Davidoff felt a fury within himself that was deeper than the fury he remembered feeling toward his own father on the day, fifty-seven years before, when the two of them, in America, had been reunited. How foolish he had been to have been seduced by memory. Never again, he thought, and as he did he found that he was standing, and talking very calmly.

"You will leave my house and you will never return," he said. "Because I never loved you as much as I wanted to. Do you understand?"

Lev left, with Gita. Sharon approached her father and when she embraced him this time, he did not resist. Doubtless, he decided, she still loved him. He lifted his arms, and held her. "My precious one," he whispered. "My child . . ." He spoke to her with great tenderness, and it pleased him to feel her body heave in spasms against his own. How wonderful it must be, he thought, to be able to weep freely.

The Golden Years

Nathan longed to return to his air-conditioned porch, but he saw that the man was there waiting for him, on the bench in front of the laundromat. He sat. The man, silver-haired and well-tanned, was bent over a yellow laundry basket, sorting empty *yahrzeit* glasses.

"So tell me," the man said. "How are you?"

"I'm here," Nathan replied.

The man laughed. "Very good," he said. He stacked glasses inside one another and moved closer to Nathan, so that their elbows touched. "That's really a terrific line—'I'm here'—but let me ask you something else: Are you sure?"

Nathan looked into the man's face—it was, as always, surprisingly handsome and boyish—and he smiled. "I think I see what you mean," he offered.

"Never," the man said, waving away Nathan's words. Nathan saw that some of the people who were waiting on line for the tram were now paying attention to them. "But listen—I suppose you're wondering about these glasses."

"Yes," Nathan said. "I was wondering about these glasses."

"I collect them," the man said, and smiled. His teeth were dazzlingly white. Nathan looked across the street at the rows of identical two-story houses—at the tile roofs, the palm trees, the flowering plants. "When it comes to *yahrzeit* glasses, this place is a real gold mine. I have at least one for every year, going all the way back to 1932, the year my father died and we lit a candle for him." He smiled again. "What I do, you see, is I stop in different people's apartments on hot days. 'I'm very thirsty,' I say to them, and one time out of three the glass they give me water in is an old *yahrzeit* glass. So then I look to see if it's one I'm still needing—I know all the special markings—and if it is, I explain my hobby to them and offer to buy the glass for a dollar, plus I give them a new *yahrzeit* glass, so they won't forget to remember the dead."

"It's an interesting hobby," Nathan said. He looked up. A long line of senior citizens on enormous tricycles, red safety flags fluttering above their heads, rode by. "I think we're attracting a crowd," Nathan whispered. He stood. He licked perspiration from his upper lip. It was a broiling August day, the temperature in the high nineties.

A tram rattled toward them, pulled by a small tractor. You could get anywhere in Century Village by using the trams—they were free—but Nathan preferred to walk. He missed Brooklyn. He missed walking along Flatbush Avenue, in their old neighborhood. He shook the man's hand. "It's been a pleasure talking to you," he said, "but I have to go now, to watch a movie being made. My brother-in-law wrote it."

"How do you like that? They're making a movie out of a play *my* brother-in-law wrote also!"

"What's his name?"

"Morris."

"My brother-in-law's name is Morris also."

"Then what's your name?" Nathan asked.

"Nachman," the man said. "And what's yours?"

"Nathan."

"Nathan—Nathan Malkin, the famous writer from Brooklyn? The author of *The Stolen Jew?*"

"Who else?"

Nathan saw that the men and women who were boarding the tram were doing so more slowly.

"But I'm Nachman Malkin, the famous *brother* from Brooklyn!"

They each took a step back, spread their arms wide, stepped forward, and embraced.

"*Brother!*" Nathan exclaimed.

"*Brother!*" Nachman exclaimed.

"Did you see their faces?" Nachman asked as they walked toward the clubhouse, each of them holding one end of the laundry basket.

"I saw," Nathan said. "Maybe you were right, years ago. Maybe everything would have worked out for the best if I'd given up my writing and we'd gone into vaudeville together."

They passed the village's main sales and rental office, then crossed a bridge. A man-made lake surrounded the island on which the clubhouse, a large two-story colonial-style building, was situated. Nathan watched the paddleboats and sailboats drifting around the lake. He thought of *The Stolen Jew*—the book he had written many years ago, when Nachman had first become ill—the story of a Jewish boy in a small village in Russia who, because of the dread *cantonist gzeyra*—the evil order—is kidnapped to take the place of another Jewish boy for twenty-five years' service in the tsar's army.

Trams were lined up side by side in front of the clubhouse. Nathan marveled at how busy, without jobs and without children, people could keep themselves here. Sewing clubs, musical groups, Talmud classes, folk dancing, mah-jongg, canasta, chess, yoga, golf, theater groups, exercise clubs, Hadassah. "In Century Village," his sister Rivka—Morris's wife—had written to him when she first arrived, "every day is Sunday." He thought of the time he and Rivka had walked across Brooklyn Bridge together on a freezing winter night carrying a bucket heavy with coal. Although Rivka was only six years old then, she had not complained. Their sister Ethel was born the next morning.

Nathan and Nachman walked around the clubhouse, showed their passes to the Burns security guard, and moved toward the shuffleboard courts. Policemen motioned them to one side, behind ropes, where hundreds of elderly people were standing, watching a movie that was being made about elderly people. A yellow crane, containing two men and a camera, rose in the air, and a man barked down orders through a megaphone.

"Come here a minute, sonny," Nachman said to a policeman. Nachman winked at Nathan. The policeman stepped toward them. "Listen. Do me a favor and take a message from me to the screenwriter Morris. Tell him we're here."

"Tell him *who's* here?" the policeman asked.

Nachman laughed. "You mean you don't recognize him?" People turned and stared. "Why he's Nathan Malkin, the famous writer. They're making his movie next. And when they do, believe me—"

"It's all right, officer," Morris said. "You can let them through."

"Where are your sunglasses?" Nathan asked.

"And your ascot?" Nachman asked.

"Jokers," Morris said. Morris took Nathan's hand in his own two hands. "But I'm very glad you came, Nathan. I want you to meet Lynn Hoffman, my director."

Nachman placed himself on one side of Morris, Nathan on the other.

"Right ball," Nachman said.

"Left ball," Nathan said.

"So who's the *schmuck* in the middle?" Nachman asked.

A man holding an enormous white placard above his head—the word "QUIET" lettered in black upon it—ran in front of them, yelling, "Quiet! Quiet!"

"*Az der rebbe shluft . . . Az der rebbe shluft . . .*" Nachman sang, softly. "*Shlufen alle chassidim . . .*"

"That was one of Poppa's favorite songs," Nathan said.

"Over here," Morris said, and he led them to folding chairs, from where they had a clear view of the shuffleboard courts. "Listen," Morris whispered. "I want you to notice the changes and tell me what you think. In the original of *The Golden Years*, if you remember, Heshel and Hannah meet through a *shitach*—Heshel's sister-in-law has them both over for a bagel-and-lox spread on Sunday morning—but in the movies, what you want are more exteriors, so we decided to have them meet while playing in a shuffleboard tournament."

Nachman groaned.

"They play alongside one another, but they can't keep their eyes on their own game," Morris continued. "It's very sweet, how the actor and actress bring it off. You'll see."

Nachman giggled. "I just had an idea," he said.

"Tell me," Nathan said.

"Do you know how much money I could lose for all of them if I wanted to run out in the middle when they start—?"

"Shh," Morris said.

"I could run out in the middle. 'I'm bored,' I could yell." Nachman looked around. "So where's shuffle—?"

The crane was moving down slowly. Then, suddenly, music filled the air. Forty elderly men on one side of the line of shuffleboard courts drew back their right arms, and—as if they were one man—they pushed and, with their shuffleboard sticks, sent round black discs gliding across the green concrete. On the other side of the court, forty elderly women, in bright gaucho pants, caught the discs with their sticks. The sound of wood knocking against wood was timed to the beat of the music. Back and forth went the round pucks of colored wood, up and down went the crane, in and out went the arms pushing the long sticks, knock knock knock went the wood—and then eighty voices filled the air:

"This is the rest of your life—
The rest of your life is here . . . !"

"*Gevalt,*" Nachman whispered, and he rested his head on Nathan's shoulder.

"We do whatever we like . . .
Without e'er a care or fear!"

"Maybe there'll be a pogrom," Nathan said.

Nachman pointed past the shuffleboard courts. "The Cossacks could come across the lake on brightly colored rafts, singing folk songs."

"Shh," Morris said. "Enough."

"Shh," Nachman said, a finger to his lips.

"Our children now all gone, we thought our lives were over—
We gave them what we could, but now it's up to them.
It's our turn now, to prance through fields of clover—
To grab in what we can—and make our lives a gem!"

A camera dollied through the lines of shuffleboard players. Seventy- and eighty-year-old men and women crossed from one side to the other, the women taking the men by the arms, the couples promenading to one side and the other as if in a square dance. Nathan thought of how he would give Hoffman his idea, of the words he would use. A microphone dangled above the head of a man in a powder-blue golf cap, and while the other players swayed and hummed behind him, the man tipped his cap toward a robust woman, and sang to her:

"This is the rest of your life,
The rest of your life is here . . .
I feel a strange kind of thrill
Right in my chest, right here—"

"Heartburn," Nachman whispered.

"*Something very new* . . ." the woman sang.

"*Something very old* . . ." the man sang.

They sang together: "*When you're only just beginning—it's hard to act so bold.*"

"Can I carry your stick back for you?" the man asked.

She handed the stick to him, and smiled. They walked down the middle of the shuffleboard courts, arm in arm.

Nathan and Nachman walked across a footbridge, from the large island to a smaller one. Platters of food—cold cuts, salads, breads, relishes—were laid out on long tables, the tables decorated with ferns and flowers. Elderly black women, in red and white aprons, stood behind the tables, serving.

"Are you hungry?" Nachman asked Morris.

"Starving," Morris said.

"Then look in a mirror and eat your heart out."

"That's an old one," Morris said.

"He knows them all," Nathan said. "It was his job, in his old life. But he's gone beyond such things now, you see. Now he believes that Jews should not be proud to have played the fool once upon a time."

"Ah," Nachman said. "In his new life then, you might say that he's been re-*Jew*-venated, is that it?"

Morris patted a place on a bench, next to him. Morris was proud, Nathan knew, that he had earned his living as a *tummler* in the Catskills years before, in an age when Grossingers consisted of a few small cottages. He enjoyed showing friends and grandchildren photographs of himself, as a young man, dressed in outlandish costumes. But after his success on Broadway with *The Golden Years*, he had made the decision to give up joke telling. Once a man who had been proud to give the guests of his hotel "never a dull moment," a man who had entertained hundreds by himself—singing, acting, dancing, falling off diving boards, slipping on banana skins, playing matchmaker—now he preferred, as he put it, to *be* entertained.

"I see what you mean," Nathan said to Nachman. "About being here or not being here."

"I dreamt I was a pickled herring," Nachman said, gazing at his plate. "And when I awoke I didn't know if I was a man who had just dreamt he was a pickled herring, or a pickled herring now dreaming he was a man."

"You shouldn't try to be such a wise guy all the time," Morris said.

Nachman stood at once and walked away.

"I'm sorry," Morris said. "But he's still difficult, Nathan. Rivka's very worried about him."

"So tell me something new."

"Something new? We're glad you're here. That's all. Maybe you can help. His theories have been multiplying lately."

"He seems in fine shape to me. We've never talked so freely with one another," Nathan said. "The truth, Morris, is that Rivka can't stand it when anyone lives without her permission."

"The way you and Nathan talk to one another, it amuses me, but what Rivka's afraid of is that maybe you'll encourage his—"

"His madness?" Nathan laughed. "Don't believe it. His madness has a life of its own. It comes and it goes when it pleases. We have little to do with it."

Nachman returned. "I'm incorrigible," he said. "So don't encourage me." He sat down next to them, his plate laden with cold cuts, pickles, and sauerkraut. He ate with his fingers.

Morris looked away. "There's Lynn," he said. Then he called: "Lynn—over here. Lynn—!"

"You shouldn't make fun all the time," Morris said. "We're all in the same boat here, really. Only instead of being poor and hungry, we're not so bad off, we eat well, and we're a little bit pushy. What should we do instead? Live like you up North, with triple locks on your doors?"

"The hospitals weren't so different," Nachman offered. "We were all in the same boat there too. We had many things in common—illness, locked doors, barred windows. We couldn't often live in cities either, or even with our own brothers and sisters, for that matter."

Morris introduced Hoffman to Nathan and Nachman. "It's a genuine pleasure," Hoffman said. "As I'm sure Morris has told you, I am a great admirer of *The Stolen Jew*."

"I'm not interested."

"And I've told Morris this too—that I think we can make a fine movie out of it—as we say in our line of work, and forgive the simplification, it would be like *Doctor Zhivago* meets *The Diary of Anne Frank*—an epic of what life was *really* like for the Jews. Because think of this, Nathan—in the movies, anything you can imagine, we can create."

"That's terrible," Nachman said. "Very depressing."

"I'm sorry," Nathan said. "I told Morris to inform you—my book is not for sale. But I do have another idea for you, Mr. Hoffman, that I brought with me from Brooklyn to Florida."

"Good," Hoffman said. "Are you free this afternoon, after shooting—let's say five o'clock?"

"I'm free," Nathan said.

"Wonderful." Hoffman started to move off, then stopped. "But I'll tell you this—I'm not taking no for an answer on *The Stolen Jew*."

Feeling as if somebody else were speaking for him, Nathan stepped toward Hoffman. "What I want to do is to make a film based upon the life of Chaim Rumkowski, elder of the Lodz ghetto," he stated. "'The Life and Death of Chaim Rumkowski, Elder of the Lodz Ghetto,' is what I would call it."

"Who?" Hoffman asked.

"*Vey iz mir*," Morris said. "Be serious, will you, Nathan? Please."

"I'm being very serious," Nathan said. "I've always been serious, except you were never listening. It would be a disaster film, you see. That's my idea. Disaster films are 'in,' as you people put it, yes? So what I was thinking was that this would be the disaster film to end all disaster films." He took a breath. "But first let me tell you about Rumkowski."

"I like it already, Nathan," Nachman said. "I knew you still had greatness left in you. Who then can say my life was in vain?"

"You're blabbering," Morris snapped. "Stop it."

"Go fuck yourself," Nachman said.

"What I have in mind is a movie so powerful that nobody will be able to stay to see the end of it," Nathan said.

Hoffman forced a laugh. "Kind of the perfect film—is that your idea, Nathan?" he asked. "So perfect that only the people who make it—the creators—will ever see it entire, right?" He let go of Nathan's hand. "Post-modernism with a vengeance."

"What I envisioned for the opening was a huge black hole in the middle of the screen," Nathan said, ignoring Hoffman, "which we realize, as the camera pulls back, is the open mouth of a child, into which a spoon with marmalade is being put. Rumkowski promised bread and marmalade to all those who volunteered for resettlement, you see. *Rescue Through Work* was his motto. *Work Saves Blood* was posted on signs throughout the ghetto."

"Rescue through retirement!" Nachman exclaimed.

"Now look," Hoffman said, easing Nathan back toward the folding chair, "if this is some kind of Holocaust film, I have to tell you right off that Holocaust films are out these days. In the first place, I couldn't get studio backing."

"No," Nathan said. "The film will take place in a ghetto, not in a concentration camp." Sweat was dripping into his eyes. Silently, he cursed himself for not having worn a hat. "The ghettos came first. I cannot imagine making a film in a death camp. That would be too easy. This is a film about living Jews, Mr. Hoffman."

Hoffman started to move away. "We'll talk later, Nathan, all right?"

Nathan reached out and grabbed Hoffman's shirt. "Or, if you don't care for marmalade, we could start the scene in the main square of Lodz, where Rumkowski addresses thousands of Jews, more Jews than there are in this entire village." He held fast to Hoffman's shirt. He stood and spoke, as if he were Rumkowski. "'Yesterday I received an order to send some twenty thousand Jews out of the ghetto. If you don't do it, they said to me, we will. And the question arose—should we do it or leave it to others.'" Nathan felt himself being pushed down. He thought he heard Hoffman's shirt tear. "'But listen to me—more important is the question not of how many we will lose, but of how many we can save!'"

"Ah!" Nachman said.

"Take it easy, Nathan," Morris said. "You look awful."

Nathan saw golf caps and sun hats. He remembered the room in the hospital where, when they were young men, he had sat and read chapters of *The Stolen Jew* to Nachman. "'Listen!'" he continued. "'I have come to the conclusion that we must accept the evil order. And I have to perform the bloody operation myself! I have to cut off limbs to save the body!'"

Nathan opened his eyes. The old people surrounding him now, with their painted hair, red lips, and bright clothing, looked like large children's dolls. "'I come like a robber, to rob your dearest ones from your very heart. With all my soul, I strove to repeal this evil order. I begged on my knees to save the children of nine and ten years old, yet I succeeded, alas, in saving only the ten-year-olds. I . . .'"

"Calm yourself, darling," Nachman was saying to him. "Calm yourself. You're overheated."

Nathan smiled at his brother. "No," he said. "I'm probably just overtired."

Nachman clapped his hands, in delight. "Momma used to say that to us all the time," he said to Morris.

"I'm an old man," Nathan said.

"You got carried away," Morris said. "It happens. You're not used to the sun. Here in Century Village I never try to write anything unless I'm inside the air-conditioning."

"My muse doesn't know from air-conditioning," Nathan said.

"She's from the old school," Nachman explained.

"I really thought he would like Rumkowski," Nathan said to Nachman. "It would be a very good part for an actor."

Nathan thought of Rumkowski riding around his ghetto in a carriage drawn by white horses. He thought of Rumkowski's portrait, on ghetto money. He thought of Rumkowski posing for murals that showed him standing guard over the sleeping ghetto, or spreading his mantle around the hungry and the children. He thought of Rumkowski drawing up elaborate schemes for a post-war Jewish utopia in which the victorious Germans would have made him king, and of Rumkowski paying poets and writers to record his acts for posterity.

"I think you scared them before, the way I used to scare people," Nachman said. "Morris didn't know what to do with you."

Nathan and Nachman sat on a bench that overlooked an inlet, and watched three swans glide across rippled water. There was a slight breeze now. Nathan could hear the sound of his own heart, and from the garden apartments to either side of them he also heard the purring of air conditioners. Nachman reached into the laundry basket and brought out a thermos of iced tea. He and Nathan drank.

"Rumkowski's ghetto was the last ghetto," Nathan explained. "So maybe he wasn't so mad. His factories produced—uniforms, shoes, gloves, furniture, even toys. The Germans needed him. And the Russians stopped seventy miles away, when they could have entered Lodz and saved the Jews. But they stopped and waited while the Germans, who knew they'd already lost the war, kept the trains to the camps running on time."

"I liked your speech very much, Nathan," Nachman said. "I want you to know that. I think it would make an excellent scene—you wouldn't even be able to watch it, it would be so terrible."

"Ah," Nathan said, feeling relaxed suddenly, and eager, once again, to share his thoughts with Nachman. "You're right, aren't you? The movies! What an advantage—to have real faces. Everything is *there*! So little is left to the imagination. You were right, Nachman. People think they have feelings in their lives because they go to the movies and they cry, but it's really the other way around, isn't it? They go to the movies to cry because they have no feelings in their lives. They cry because the movies tell them to cry. It's what they pay for. It's very hard to feel nothing when you see what looks like an actual human being experience what appears to be actual joy or suffering. So you cry and you tell yourself, 'See—I must be human. I cried.'"

"I wouldn't know," Nachman said, looking away. "I stopped going to movies the week before my Bar Mitzvah. Remember when we saw *Bambi* together, and I cried so much the matron came and made you take me home?"

"Yes," Nathan said.

"That's why I think your idea is so wonderful," Nachman said. "A movie that you wouldn't be able to sit through is the kind of movie I was made for."

"You're my ideal audience, I suppose," Nathan said.

"But listen—do you want a real secret?"

"Of course. Only take your time. Don't get carried away the way I did."

Nachman waved a hand at him. "Me?—I was carried away years ago! But listen—the secret I was thinking of giving you was this, that when you were a boy and you ran away from home—remember?—and everybody worried about you for doing such a thing, what I hoped was that you would die and that people would love me for the heroic way I endured your loss."

Nachman stopped and waited, but Nathan said nothing.

"You're not angry?"

"It's a good secret," Nathan said, touching his brother's hand. "Only you didn't need to save it for so long."

Sirens wailed. Nathan watched elderly people—in trams, in their patios—freeze, and look toward the ambulance, its red light flashing.

"You meant *my* loss, before," Nathan said. He stood and began to walk. "You said *your* loss."

"Is it true that Jews ate each other in the ghettos?" Nachman asked.

"Yes."

"Good," Nachman said. "That's a help with one of my theories."

"Which is?"

"I was reading a book where they ran an experiment—they trained mice to do certain tricks and then they killed them and chopped up their brains and fed the brains to another group of mice. Then they took this group and tried to teach them the same tricks and they took another group which they fed normally, and it turned out that the mice who ate the brains learned the trick faster." Nachman paused. "It's connected to a theory I have about the survival of the Jews."

Nathan smiled, and thought of his empty house, in Brooklyn, where he had grown up with Nachman and their two sisters. Once, nearly fifty years earlier, when the rooms were all occupied, he recalled, he had dreamt of writing seven different books at the same time, one in each room of the house. Every morning, he thought, he would start in one room and work on that room's story for an hour or so. Then he would leave that room and go into the next, and work on that room's story. The idea had been returning to him recently, and he realized that it appealed to him even more now, at this end of his life, than it had when he was young. If he returned north, to Brooklyn, and if he worked on each book for an hour each day, and took an hour off for lunch, and if...

The *American Sun & Wind* Moving Picture Company

In the forest, high above the lake, I imagined that I was, far below, trapped beneath the black ice. I gathered sticks for kindling, pressed them close to my chest, then brought the bundle, like a gift, to the edge of the woods. I saw that Mr. Lesko and his horse were already out on the ice, clouds of steam pouring from the horse's nostrils.

Beside the small fire, my uncle Max was unwrapping the camera from its blanket—lifting it tenderly, as if it were an infant—then setting it upon the tripod: a sign that we would soon begin. I closed my eyes and prayed that I wasn't too late—that I had not stayed in the forest too long, and that there was still time for me to help make up our new story.

I could make a story out of anything—a nail, a glass, a shoe, a tree, a mirror, a button, a window, a wall—and for every story I made up and gave away, I also made one up I told no one about—one I stored inside me, in the rooms where I kept my most precious memories and pictures.

Below me, Mr. Lesko was hitching his horse to the ice plow and, when he urged his horse forward, I climbed into his head and saw that he was hoping the horse would resist him so that he might use his whip. The sleighs—pungs, we called them—were on land, next to the ice house, and while I was gone, Mr. Lesko and his son had cut a runway into the lake's shallow end, for floating the cakes of ice to shore.

I closed my eyes, made a picture of the lake, and labeled the picture as if I were back at our studio, printing out an opening title for one of the moving pictures my family made:

FORT LEE, NEW JERSEY
NOVEMBER 12, 1915

I opened my eyes and saw that my uncle Max was fishing inside his suitcase for his lenses and film. My mother was lifting dresses and hats from the clothing bag my father held open for her. My uncle Karl was talking with Mr. Lesko, showing him where he wanted the ice cut.

I made my way down the hill and started across the lake to where the fire was burning below the camera. I had helped build it there—lit the first match to the greasy newspapers so that, the heat rising steadily, the oil in the camera would remain soft and the gears would not freeze.

I looked into the black ice—the first ice of winter—veined like marble, clear like glass. In the space between land and snow, I knew, small animals and insects lived all winter long. I wondered if there were a space like that between water and ice, where I might lie down.

In ancient times, Max taught me, men would build memory palaces inside their minds, and in each of the palace's rooms they would keep furniture, and on the furniture they would place objects. They invented systems and conjured up images by which they could name the rooms, and recall which rooms contained which objects and how the rooms led to and from one another. Sometimes they did this to remember the objects themselves, and sometimes the objects were there to remind them of other objects, or of lists or texts they wanted to set to heart—of the words to the Psalms, or the names of the saints, or where all the stars in the universe were located.

In our own times, Max said, people still organized their memories in similar ways, but now instead of being kings, priests, or philosophers living in temples and palaces, they were magicians, memory artists, and *idiot savants* working in vaudeville, at county fairs, or in circuses.

My father's three suitcases, like steps leading to an invisible stage, sat side by side on the ice, next to the sleds on which we transported our equipment, and inside the suitcases were his accordion, his violin, and his clarinet. When Karl wanted actors and actresses to show more feeling, he had my father play for them. My father played his violin during love scenes. He played his accordion during barroom scenes and cowboy movies. He played his clarinet, his flute, or small pump-organ for night scenes, or when people were dying.

I deposited my bundle of sticks next to the fire. Max tapped the side of the camera. Is this one reel? he asked.

No, I said. It's not real until you open the shutter, turn the handle, and let the light inside.

Stop with the nonsense, Karl said. Two reels, he said. This one's a two-reeler we gotta finish by the end of the week.

Max winked at me. But if it's *too* real, I asked, how will we be able to bear it?

And we don't need your crappy routines either, you two, Karl snapped. If I want your opinion, I'll give it to you.

Leave the boy alone, my father said. He's a good boy, even if he looks like a girl.

Mr. Lesko's son was on the ice now too, but I could not tell which was the father and which the son. They both wore beaver coats, the fur turned to the inside, and black leather hats with earlaps. One of them walked on the far side of the horse, pushing an ice-marker back and forth along the surface of the lake, making a checkerboard of squares.

Max's warm breath was on my face. Joey? he asked.

I closed my eyes. I see a woman drowning, I said.

Karl came closer. And—? he asked. Okay. So she's drowning. So what else—?

I see her drowning, I said, and she's caught inside a hole in the ice, trying to climb out, to save herself.

And then—? Karl asked.

There's a man, and he has a whip in his hand. I looked up at the hill where I had been a short while before, and I pointed. And there's a frightened child up there, alone in the forest.

Why? Max asked.

Because the woman had to marry the man after she gave birth to the child. But the man beat the child, and one day, when it was old enough, it ran away.

I like it, Karl said. This we can sell—whips, and a mother and child we can weep for, and then a chase.

Whipping and weeping, my father said brightly. We all looked at him. He shrugged. Whoopee, he added, softly.

My mother put her arm around his neck. Shh, she said. She looked toward me. What else, sweetheart?

Well, there's another man, I think, and he looks exactly like the man with the whip, except that his eyes are different. This man is the man she truly loves, and he's running through the forest as fast as he can.

The horse! Karl said. Come on with the horse before I freeze my nuts off.

But why a horse? Max asked.

Why a horse?! Karl exclaimed. Because we've *got* a horse—that's why!

Sure, my father said. Do the best with what you've got and leave the rest to God. That's what I always say.

My philosopher, my mother said, then kissed my father, laughed, reached inside her coat, pulled out a pistol, and fired it at the sky.

Come on and get me, you dirty varmints! she cried out.

I hugged her hard. *I've got you!* I shouted.

My little baby Joey, she whispered. My angel boy. Don't ever let them hurt you. Promise me, all right?

I promise, I said.

My mother was the most beautiful woman in the world when she got like this—going from hot to cold, from anger to love to sadness and back again. She held me at a distance. Such a sweet nose, she said. She tugged once on each of my ears, then lifted my cap and roughed my hair. What a waste, what a waste. Maybe your father's right—that you should have been a girl.

My father took me from her, lifted me high in the air. Get a load of those tiny ears, he said. And those gorgeous curls.

Shh, Max said. He's a boy, not a girl. Leave him be.

Hurry! Karl said. We gotta hurry. Look! Karl pointed to the far end of the lake, where, behind the northern range of low, rolling hills, a wide, black wall of clouds rose up like a mountain. The clouds moved toward us as if the ocean were behind them, pushing them through the sky.

The Leskos pulled chisels from their overcoats, knelt down and started hammering and chopping along the lines they had made with their ice-marker. Karl slapped at his shoulders and walked in circles around the fire, first one way, and then the other.

This is why I'm moving to California, he said. All right? In California we can make movies every day of the year without freezing our tushes off. In California, Edison and his thugs won't burn down our studio and break our cameras. Everyone else is out there already. Griffith's making features he's gonna charge two bucks a seat for—two bucks, for crying out loud!—and I'm still pissing my life away with these two-reelers.

Max cupped his palm over my eyes. Joey? he asked.

I see a horse falling through the ice, I said. The woman and the child are holding on to the horse and the two men who look the same are trying to pull them from the ice. And there's blood. I see lots of blood, and it's turning the water black.

Terrific, Karl said. Love, danger, violence, rescue—we stick to the basics. That's terrific, Joey. Really terrific. So okay. So one of you geniuses tell me—where do we start?

Inside the icehouse, my mother said.

Why the icehouse? Karl asked.

So we can get warm, my mother said. Then she started running across the ice in long strides, gliding and making believe her boots were ice skates. She jumped over the open runway, stopped, put more bullets into the chamber of her pistol, spun the chamber, clicked it closed. She was having one of her wild days, when you never knew what she would do next. She turned toward us and shouted, as if she were leading a cavalry charge: Ready or not, here we come—The American Sun & Wind Moving Picture Company!

Then she fired her gun into the air, three times, and the explosions blasted through my skull like the sound the lake would make if it were splitting open. I heard a man scream. The Leskos were trying to control their horse, which was hammering the air with its hooves. The screaming came from the hilltop where I had been standing a few minutes before. A man stood there now, his hands clasped above his heart.

Holy mackerel! my mother said. I finally did it.

Max! Karl yelled. Start shooting—we'll figure out the story later. Hurry, Max. Camera! Camera!

Max did what Karl told him to, while the man on the hill, hands pressed to his heart, twirled in a circle, tumbled down the slope, rolling this way and that so that I was afraid his skull would smash against boulders and tree trunks.

It's Izzie! my father shouted, clapping his hands. I watched Izzie carom off a rock, sail onto the ice and spin around, face down. He lay there for a few seconds, as if dead, and I ran toward him.

When I was no more than ten feet away, he stood up, grinned, doffed his cap, and bowed.

Hurray for Izzie! I yelled.

Izzie was my mother's cousin, our stunt man when he was sober, and often when he was not. He could walk on the ledges of high buildings, stand on the wings of flying airplanes, jump out of burning windows, and ride wild horses. He could duel with swords, drive cars like a maniac, and fight with his fists like Battling Levinsky.

How's my favorite little guy? he asked, and before I could answer, he hoisted me into the air and was racing across the ice with me. I stretched my legs and arms way out, as if I were an airplane. We zoomed in for a landing, and he set me down beside the fire and started in kissing my mother.

My father grabbed Izzie and began waltzing him around in circles while he sang the words to "The Beautiful Blue Danube."

Karl was screaming through his megaphone that time was money, that we were robbing him blind, that by the time we finished shooting in the icehouse and got back out here, we'd have lost our light.

Easy does it, cousin, Izzie said, his arm around Karl's shoulder. Like I always say, the main thing in life is to have a good time and not to get hurt. Everything else is extra.

Not to get hurt? Karl shot back. Ha! I think maybe what we got here is a major case of the pot calling the kettle black.

I never risk injury, Izzie said, and he repeated words he always gave to people when they told him he took chances: Everything I do in this life is figured out exactly.

The Leskos put away their chisels. One of them took a pair of ice tongs from the leather harness on the side of the horse, opened the tongs wide, hooked them into the cake of ice. But even before they lifted out the first cake, I realized that only some of the blood in the lake was coming from where the horse was scraping its neck and legs raw against the sharp edges of ice.

Izzie rubbed his hands together. So what are we waiting for? Let's put this show on the road.

But what if it rains or it snows? my father asked. We have to think about that also. What if there's a storm? What do we do then?

We shoot our moving picture, Karl said, whether it rains, whether it snows, whether it storms, or whether it stinks.

My father lifted his accordion, shrugged the straps into place over his shoulders, began playing "My Bonnie Lies over the Ocean." My mother reached into the small telescope bag in which she kept her make-up, took out her mirror and her lipstick, passed the gold tube back and forth through the flames to thaw it, then lifted the lid and twisted the tube of red wax upwards. She stacked my father's suitcases to eye level, set her mirror on top, and began doing her lips.

I saw fountains of blood explode from the bottom of the lake. The wind was roaring through the water like thunder, tearing holes in whatever was in its way—rocks, animals, trees, children—and I closed my eyes again, the way I did when I wanted a scene to change, and I saw that below the ice, water, and mud, an entire lost world existed—cities, buildings, castles, people—and that it was from this world that the blood was rising.

Here, sweetheart, my mother said. It's time. She handed me the mirror and the lipstick, so that, for our story, I could begin to make myself into her daughter.

I looked at my image in the mirror—stared through the dark holes in the middle of my eyes and imagined that on the wall at the back of my skull, my face, like the pictures inside Max's camera, was upside down.

So tell me, Joey, Izzie asked. Would you like to be our director? He handed me Karl's megaphone. Taped to the wide end of the funnel was a circle of cardboard, and in the middle of the cardboard my uncle had cut out a rectangle, so his megaphone could double as a viewfinder. I looked through his viewfinder at my mother, squinting until the only thing I could see was her lips. They were wine-red and moist, and someday soon they would fill entire screens—forty feet wide and thirty feet high in the theaters in New York City.

The boy wants to be a director, Izzie said.

Fine with me, Karl said. I had enough already for a lifetime. Take over. He's got my blessing.

Good. So here comes everything you need to know, Izzie said. Are you ready?

Ready, I said.

Okay. Then repeat after me—Camera.

Camera!

Action.

Action!

Cut.

Cut!

Now you know everything Karl knows, he said, and he kissed me hard on the mouth. Now you're a director.

The Leskos were floating cakes of ice along the runway, toward shore. I held a strip of black velvet up, next to the camera. When my mother turned and looked at it, her pupils dilated, and her pale blue eyes went dark.

Cut! Karl said, and Max stopped shooting. My mother looked away. I put the strip of velvet in my pocket, and while Max counted, I back-cranked the camera for him, eight turns. Then he tilted the camera down, its lens pointed at the open water, and he cranked the handle forward, so that before one scene ended the next would begin. That way my mother's eyes would seem to dissolve in the dark water of the lake. You would see her face, aflame with fear, and then you would see her eyes grow dark with despair, after which the scene would melt, and you would move right through her eyes until you were staring into water as deep and black as the night.

One of the Leskos hooked a cake of ice with a pike pole, dragged the cake onto a plank. When the Leskos had six cakes of ice lined up, they jammed them together, shoved a slab of wood into them at one end—there were two metal spikes in the wood—attached the slab of wood to the horse by rope, and made the horse pull the blocks of ice along the plank, to shore.

By this time the Leskos had carved out a section of the lake that was as large and square as the infield diamond of a baseball field. Max raised his camera slowly, set it in position, and photographed the northern crescent of the lake where Mr. Lesko was walking behind his horse, plowing the ice. Mr. Lesko played my mother's cruel husband.

Mr. Lesko's son played The Gentle Stranger. He wore a ragged brown wool coat Izzie had given him, and he worked without a hat, so that the winter light, playing through his curls from behind, made him appear very gentle.

I was wearing a wig made of real hair—long auburn tresses—and under my black coat, on top my regular clothes, I now had on a white blouse and a blue pinafore.

Action! Karl shouted through his megaphone.

Mr. Lesko stopped plowing, took out his whip, raised it above his shoulder.

Camera! Karl shouted.

Max began cranking, and Mr. Lesko started whipping his horse.

No! I screamed. And I shot out from where I stood, streaked across the ice, grabbed at his arm. He threw me off easily.

Cut! Karl shouted.

Wonderful, Joey! he called. That was wonderful! I didn't expect you to do that.

I had not expected to do it either, but I didn't say so.

Izzie took the whip from Mr. Lesko's hand, raised it high in the air, as if he were going to strike him, but instead he pivoted and lashed out at the horse. The whip cracked, making a sound like a bullet firing, but the lash never touched the horse's flank.

This is your last warning, Izzie said. If you whip the horse again, I'll whip you. Is that clear? And you *never* touch the boy.

Mr. Lesko said nothing.

Izzie scares me with his anger, my mother said. He never used to be so angry.

He needs a drink, my father said. He always gets this way when he needs a drink. I watched Izzie squat down and dip his hand in the water, to test its coldness. I watched Mr. Lesko coil his whip. I watched my father take out a small pair of scissors with which he snipped the fingers from a pair of wool gloves so that, the pink tips of his fingers exposed, he could continue to play his instruments in the cold.

Behind the clouds, the light in the sky was starting to fade, and I imagined sitting with my mother on a ledge of ice, above the open channel, after everyone else was gone. I imagined us slipping quietly over the edge, descending noiselessly through water, and passing through the lake's sandy bottom. I had given them one story and now I was making up another, one I could keep inside me forever—about how my mother and I made our way into the lost world below the lake, where we found out the source of all the howling and blood.

Max photographed Mr. Lesko's eyes, and then he photographed the horse's eyes. Next he photographed Mr. Lesko's son, who was using tongs to lift blocks of ice from the plank onto the sleigh. When Mr. Lesko's son looked at his father, his eyes became soft, like the eyes of a wounded animal.

Brilliant! Karl said, peering through his viewfinder. You're a genius, Joey, to have thought of making the husband and the lover the same man.

Their faces are the same, but their eyes are opposite, Max said.

Yes, Karl said. You can make miracles with eyes, Max—I gotta hand you that. In life, you see, eyes are just little things in a face, with skin that goes up and down over them, but in moving pictures, the eyes—oh the eyes are everything.

Max unscrewed the camera and wrapped it in a blanket. I helped load the sleds with our equipment, and then we walked back across the ice, up onto land, through the snow, to the icehouse.

Our story that day was simple, and we made it up as we went along the way we always did.

My mother was living a harsh and lonely life, married to Mr. Lesko and caring for me, her beloved daughter. In early scenes, which we would shoot back at our studio the next day and then patch in later, you would see the two of us slaving away for Mr. Lesko in his kitchen, and submitting to his tyranny, until the day upon which The Gentle Stranger wandered into our world.

The Gentle Stranger owned a book of poems, and in the evenings, when our chores were done, he read to us from Tennyson, Swinburne, and Shelley. Karl liked to put sections of poems into the titles because if the pictures didn't tell people what to feel, he said, the words would.

Max disagreed. He believed our stories should be told in pictures only, so that anyone in the world, in any time and place, could understand them. Because all the stories I made up came to me in a series of pictures that marched across the screen inside my head—pictures that seemed less real the instant I even *tried* to find words to describe them—I agreed with Max.

We think in pictures, Max always said. Not words.

Even though I agreed with him, whenever I found pictures and people in my head I wanted to save, I gave them names, the way I named The Gentle Stranger, and I invented titles to put on the doors and windows of their rooms, so that someday, if I wanted to, I would be able to find them again.

The Gentle Stranger Finds a New Home
With the Mother and Her Love-Child

In exchange for food and lodging, The Gentle Stranger worked for Mr. Lesko, cutting wood and harvesting ice. Mr. Lesko let him use the icehouse for a home, and he slept there at night, wrapped in old blankets, between walls of ice and sawdust.

Then one night, after Mr. Lesko got drunk and fell asleep, we stole away to the icehouse, and my mother told The Gentle Stranger our story: how she had been sent to work for Mr. Lesko as a housekeeper, and how Mr. Lesko had forced himself upon her, after which, in her shame, she had had no choice but to become his wife.

Perhaps it was God's will, my mother said, drawing me close to her. For had I not submitted to Mr. Lesko, my most precious jewel would not be here.

That was when The Gentle Stranger declared his love for my mother. He went down on his knees and clasped my mother's hands. I have never loved another as I love you, he said. You have rescued me from the dead. Without you I cannot live.

My mother's true heart showed in her eyes, but she pulled her hands free and turned away.

I am a married woman, she said.

I looked at The Gentle Stranger and I looked at my mother. I took his hand and I took hers—the hand on which she wore her wedding band—and I joined their hands together.

Then we argued.

Karl said that next my mother and The Gentle Stranger should plan to murder Mr. Lesko—to arrange for an accident, where he drowned in the lake.

My father said that the three of us should just run away together and start a new life. Let love reign triumphant! he said.

Oh Simon, my mother said, and she rested her head on my father's shoulder. You're the dearest man in the world, aren't you?

I like happy endings that make me cry, my father said.

Izzie said the problem was that we didn't know who The Gentle Stranger was and why he was there and why he was saved from the dead. If they killed Mr. Lesko, they'd get caught and go to jail and I'd be an orphan. Why, he asked, should people pay good money to see lives that were more miserable than their own?

Izzie's right, my father said.

I said that maybe The Gentle Stranger had originally come to the lake intending to commit suicide. When he looked into the water, however, he had seen, not his own reflection, but that of my mother, and seeing her eyes, he had decided to live.

Max beamed, said we could start with the scene in the icehouse—of them holding hands—and then go to a dream-like flashback, by using a piece of fine gauze over the lens, of The Gentle Stranger staring at my mother's image in the water—her fingers clasped together in prayer, her hands themselves seeming to dissolve, only to reappear and rise up, as if disembodied, from the depths of the lake.

In addition to which, Izzie said, who would ever believe a square hole in an ice-covered lake was natural? Everyone would think we were tricking them with miniatures and false shots we'd cooked up in the studio.

Karl said the story was getting too complicated and too expensive. He asked my opinion, and I suggested we combine the two stories: The Gentle Stranger and my mother could still plot to murder Mr. Lesko—but because they were incapable of such an act, they could also change their minds at the last minute.

And then, Karl said, just when they change their minds—I got it, I got it!—there can be a terrible accident that kills Mr. Lesko anyway.

Except that, because they planned the murder, I said, nobody will believe it was an accident, and they'll be made to suffer forever for what they did *not* do.

Because we were going to shoot indoors, Max changed to the longest of his three lenses and set the aperture wide open. To make use of the available light, we kept the door of the icehouse open and set up a clothesline between two trees, a stiff white bedsheet hanging from it to reflect light into the house. Later, Karl said, we would tint this part of the film blue, to transform it into night.

Max could mix wonderful colors—gold for dawn, yellow for candlelight, red for war scenes, peach-glow for sunsets—and sometimes, late at night in the old trolley barn we had converted into our studio and home, he would let me bathe the strips of film in dyes and choose the colors we would use, not just to indicate the time of day, as now, or, by adding color to the usual black-and-white stock, to emphasize what was happening—the way we did for battles and weddings—but to create the atmosphere that helped you understand the *feelings* in the scenes: pale blues for sadness, glowing ambers for peacefulness, crimsons for passion, ruby reds for lust, forest greens for happiness.

But the colors for feelings—unlike the colors for night, war, dawn, fire, sunsets, and candlelight—were never fixed. Sometimes forest green could show how happy our people were, while at other times it could reveal their fear. Sometimes bathing a scene in indigo could let you sense the joy the characters were experiencing, and sometimes it helped you to feel that the actors and actresses were merely, like the color itself, blue.

As soon as Karl had arranged the scene the way he wanted, in the icehouse, my mother wrapped me in a cloak, and gave me a basket of food, a letter placed at the bottom of the basket, to take to The Gentle Stranger, who was hiding in the forest, waiting for us.

But if you meet in the forest, how would the accident take place on the lake? Karl asked. I told you before—we got a lake, we use a lake.

Okay, Izzie said. This is how it works. We cut through the rope so when he's chasing them through the forest with his horse and sleigh, the rope snaps, the sleigh throws him off flying, and he goes tumbling down the hill into the water.

But we have to figure out how it becomes an accident instead of murder, Karl said.

Maybe it's the opposite of the Red Sea, my father said. Maybe the lake closes shut with ice, and then it opens again and he falls in, splash!

Good, Simon, Izzie said. Terrific. So we chop out a chunk of ice and tow it in, and then we tow it back out. You can show me floating in the lake, face down, in Mr. Lesko's coat and his hat, like I'm drowned, and then the child pokes me with the pike pole, and turns me over and I'll give you a look from underwater that will make people freeze in their seats.

Izzie began smearing his arms and legs with grease, for when he would be drowning in the lake, and while he did I remembered the first picture I had seen inside my head, with which I had begun our story, of a woman drowning, only I didn't understand how that was to come true any more, since we had changed things and decided that Mr. Lesko would be the one to drown.

As soon as Mr. Lesko found my mother's letter and read it, he took out his whip. My mother crawled backwards across the snow, to the icehouse, her forearm across her eyes. Mr. Lesko's arm came flashing down and I leapt in front of my mother, covering her body with my own. The whip's lash cut into my cheek, and the burning sensation—warm and liquid—felt wonderful.

I had not known that this would happen.

Before my mother could tend to me, Izzie had lifted Mr. Lesko from the ground and was pounding him against the side of the icehouse. Mr. Lesko's son lifted a pike pole and tried to stab Izzie, but Izzie saw him coming and stepped aside.

The pike pole rammed into Mr. Lesko's side.

Keep shooting, Karl said. Keep shooting. We'll cut it all up later.

They're cut up now, my father said. He put down his accordion and packed handfuls of snow onto the side of my face. Izzie reached inside his coat, pulled out a leather-covered flask, and took a long drink. He shouldn't drink while he works, my father said.

Don't drink while you work, my mother said.

If I need a wife, I'll buy one, Izzie snapped.

Falling into the lake will sober him up, my father said. Everything Izzie does is figured out exactly.

We moved to the top of the hill and Max set up his camera there, first to show us racing through the forest to warn The Gentle Stranger that Mr. Lesko was coming to do him harm—and then to show Mr. Lesko charging through the forest with his horse and sleigh.

We photographed my mother sawing through the horse's reins with a kitchen knife. We photographed us changing our mind, and trying to tie the reins back together, but before we could, Mr. Lesko, believing we were trying to escape, beat us away with his whip.

So we fled into the forest, past Max's camera, and it felt wonderful to run across the frozen ground, holding tight to my mother's hand, my curled tresses flying out behind me, the frigid air kissing my cheek and sealing the blood there. Izzie put on Mr. Lesko's coat and hat and shoved Mr. Lesko from the sleigh. Mr. Lesko tried to stop him—to tell him he had not finished tying the reins back together—but Izzie knocked him to the ground.

Izzie rode away, then turned back. Max photographed me and my mother slipping down the hill, hand in hand, to the lake. The Gentle Stranger stood in the middle of the lake, waiting for us, but where our camera had been, jagged slabs of ice now floated like small islands. Our plan was to jump from island to island, toward the south end of the lake, where there was a waterfall.

Max could photograph us from the other side of the waterfall and, even though we would be nowhere near the falls, he could foreshorten the distance and make it appear we were in danger of plunging over, to our death.

Max photographed Izzie, disguised as Mr. Lesko, speeding across the snow in his horse and sleigh. Then he moved his camera back onto the ice and photographed me and my mother running along the shore until we found a place from which to step out onto the ice. The fire on the lake was gone and Max said we had to hurry, for the cold air could cause flashes of static electricity inside the camera.

My mother and I set out across the lake, and we called to The Gentle Stranger.

Izzie started down the hill. I saw that the real Mr. Lesko was smiling, and I called out to Izzie to be careful. The reins! I called. The reins!

It doesn't matter, my father said. You heard Karl. Whether it rains or it snows or it stinks, we shoot.

But it was too late. The reins snapped. The horse buckled, as if its forelegs had been chopped off. It tumbled downhill, crashed into a tree, and kept rolling. The sleigh skidded on a single runner in an opposite direction. Izzie leapt out, but he had not planned to do so at that spot, and though he avoided crashing into a tree, he landed hard, shoulder first, against a boulder, and spun upside down, in a somersault, clutching at his shoulder.

Wonderful! Karl called out through his megaphone.

My father pulled at the rope that was hooked into the slab of ice we were riding on, so that at the exact moment when the horse reached the shore, the ice moved, and the horse fell directly into water, its head cracking against the ice's edge.

I heard a sound come from its neck, like that of a tree snapping in high wind.

In the open water, the blood pooled.

Izzie rolled into the water behind the horse.

Mr. Lesko stopped smiling. He held to his side, where Izzie had rammed the pike pole, as if it were only now that he felt the pain. His horse thrashed at the water, trying to climb out, and the more wildly it thrashed, the more the blood in the water foamed.

My mother watched Izzie lift his hand, grasp at air, then sink beneath the water's bubbling skin. Her eyes rolled up in their sockets. She fainted, and lay across our island of ice, one leg caught under her, her hair trailing in the water.

The Gentle Stranger came toward us, leaping from island to island, as if to rescue me and my mother, but when he got to us, he plunged straight into the water and grabbed for the horse's reins.

From the shore, Mr. Lesko walked into the lake.

Where's Izzie? my father asked. He cupped his hands around his mouth, and called out: Izzie—! Oh Izzie! Where *are* you?

The horse floated up and rolled onto its side.

Then Izzie rose to the surface. Shit, he said. It's colder than a pair of witch's tits down there.

Suddenly, the horse rose up from the water, above Izzie, as if it were about to fly.

The horse! I cried. The horse!

Izzie turned, but too late, and the horse dropped down upon him with its full weight. Izzie disappeared beneath the horse and the water. The horse had one hoof on our island of ice, but the hoof slipped and the horse fell backwards, its neck catching on a point of the ice, the ice tearing out a long gash and stripping the skin away. As if sprung from a trap, a splintered bone shot through the exposed flesh.

Mr. Lesko waded through the water as if he were walking through brambles.

We have to save them, Max said.

Keep shooting, Karl said. Don't stop.

But they could die, Max said. This is really happening.

Luck! Karl said. Sometimes, after you give up all hope, and when you least expect it, you get lucky. Go figure.

Izzie appeared behind us, climbed onto our island. I think the horse is dead, he said.

See? Karl said. When it comes to stunts, Izzie never takes chances. Keep shooting, Max. Only leave Mr. Lesko out of the frame. We can't have two husbands show up in the same scene.

My mother opened her eyes. You're alive, she said to me. You're alive!

My mother stood. And you too, she said to Izzie, but when she moved to embrace him, Mr. Lesko, struggling in water where he could no longer stand, snatched at her ankle.

My mother tumbled over the island's edge, into the water.

Wonderful! Karl said.

That wasn't supposed to happen, my father said.

Yes it was, Karl said. Don't you remember what Joey said about seeing a woman drowning, about the woman and the child holding to the horse, about the horse in the water?

Ah! my father said. You're right again.

So I dove into the water to rescue my mother. I saw her dark hair floating through the blood, and I reached out, closed my hands around the hair, but at that instant the horse rolled up between us, as if it were a huge barrel, and I found myself holding to the horse's blood-drenched mane.

Mr. Lesko's son was on the shore now, tying a rope to the reins, and pulling. I turned and saw pink water drip from the corner of my mother's mouth. Her eyelids moved up, globes of milk-white gelatin like those we set before the projector's lens rolling where her blue eyes had been.

I felt as if my chest were being crushed between walls of thick limestone. Mr. Lesko and his son pulled steadily on the rope, to haul their horse from the water.

My mother's mouth was open, and her lips were white. In the camera, I thought, black was white and white was black. In my mother's telescope bag there would still be a perfect, red impression of her mouth, on tissue, where she had blotted it.

The storm is here, my father said, pointing to the sky.

We have to help them, Max said. They'll get frostbite. They'll lose their toes, their fingers.

Keep shooting, Karl said. It's even better than what the boy saw. It's real!

Then nobody will believe it, my father said.

Max left the camera, grabbed blankets from the ground—the blankets in which he kept his spools of film and extra lenses—and he rushed toward us.

Make a fire, he said to my father. Make a fire. Quickly.

Karl took Max's place and cranked the camera's handle.

If we don't use it now, we'll use it later, he said. Nothing is wasted. Nothing is lost.

I climbed out of the water. My teeth were clicking like dice. Max wrapped me in a blanket, and began rubbing my cheeks with his hands.

You have the heart of a murderer, Max said to Karl.

Don't make me laugh, Karl said. Did I cut the reins? Did I shove them in the water? Did I kill the horse?

Izzie emerged from the water, my mother in his arms. He set her down on the snow, covered her with blankets, put a flask of whiskey to her lips.

Listen, my brave brother, Karl said to Max. Did *you* leap into the water to save them?

The horse lay on its side, blood spilling from its mouth as if a long strip of red film were unfurling from its innards.

Mr. Lesko pried open the horse's teeth and blood shot out onto his face as if pumped from a fire hose.

The horse twitched, pawed the air with its hooves.

Suddenly my mother stood up, as if she were neither wet, nor cold, nor frightened. She reached under her coat and took out her pistol.

She went to the horse, put the muzzle of the pistol to its forehead, and fired twice.

Mr. Lesko and his son went down on their knees. They each made the sign of the cross. Above us, the dark clouds were lower than the hills, separating and spreading now as if, like thin, soiled cloth, the sky itself were rotting.

Mr. Lesko bent his head, pressed it against the horse's neck, and wept.

Cut! Karl said. Cut! We got it.

LITERARY MODERNISM SERIES

Thomas F. Staley, *editor*

Books by Jay Neugeboren

FICTION

Big Man

Listen Ruben Fontanez

Corky's Brother (stories)

Sam's Legacy

An Orphan's Tale

The Stolen Jew

Before My Life Began

Poli: A Mexican Boy in Early Texas

Don't Worry about the Kids (stories)

NONFICTION

Parentheses: An Autobiographical Journey

The Story of STORY Magazine (editor)

Imagining Robert: My Brother, Madness, and Survival

Transforming Madness: New Lives for People Living with Mental Illness

Open Heart: A Patient's Story of Life-Saving Medicine and Life-Giving Friendship

The Hillside Diary and Other Writings (editor)